ISBN 979-8-9858332-5-6 (paperback)

Published by Forever Inspired Publishing

Double Tap:
All is Fair in Love and War

Double Tap:
All is Fair in Love and War

Written by D'Angelo Tucker

One to the head, One to the heart ....

Golden sand glittering like a trillion diamonds sparkle under the summer sun. Foam filled ocean waves slap the shores of the beach temporarily transforming the dry gritty surface to soft and slick before the lingering heat restores the granules. A warm breeze deposits sand onto the balcony of a lavish modern marvel of architectural design, a true work of art. Molded metal, crafted concrete, slate and stone. The perfect dream home with the perfect view.

Chapter 1
Blood and Water

Ownership of this astonishing residence is split down the middle 50/50 between a set of identical twin brothers, William and Warren Love. William a.k.a Will is the reserved one. Quiet, clean cut. A man of few words. Observative, calculating, the type of person that would make a game of chess challenging the best minds of the sport while his brother Warren a.k.a War is the complete polar opposite. A wild man, reckless, fearless, outgoing, and outspoken; the life of the party.

He completely lives up to his name. He's impulsive where Will is cautious. Daring when Will sticks to his carefully laid plans. Their dissimilarities are as obvious as night and day, but the bond these brothers share is one that runs deep and can never be broken. The combining of both personalities makes for the perfect hit squad. They were introduced into this world sharing a womb and for these two, it's been them against the world until the day they share a tomb.

Will stirred out of his sleep to the rhythmic thudding sounds resonating from the other wing of the house. His eyes were still closed but without seeing it, he knew what it was. Checking the alarm clock the display read 6:38 a.m. Will exhaled with a slight annoyance and sat up swinging his legs around to the edge of the bed, planting his feet on the plush inviting carpet that covered his bedroom floor. Beside him was a half-drunk glass of water that he finished in two gulps and set the empty glass back down on the coaster of a spotless nightstand. Will's room was immaculately clean like a hospital; everything was in its place. He stretched and yawned before lazily staggering to his bathroom to get his day started. He and his brother had business to attend to.

On the other end of the mansion War was waking up as well, but to one of three stunningly attractive unfamiliar women, planting soft kisses on his neck while tracing his nipples with her fingertips. One of the other women used the tip of her tongue as a wet marker and traced the line of his happy trail all the way down War's abdomen, unleashing a devilish grin before she disappeared beneath the covers. War groaned with delight as he allowed the young lady to have her way with him, watching her head bobbing up and down under the sheets for a while before he yanked the covers back.

He had reached the point during the escapade where he needed to watch. After a while the third young lady joined in.

By this time, it was too much to remain still as he flipped over one onto their back pinning her down and feasting on her vagina hungrily before sliding in her. War furiously pounded her while the other two women watched on, anxiously awaiting their turns.

War's room was disorganized and chaotic, just how he liked it. Empty beer cans and alcohol bottles were on every tabletop and nightstand surface. An amalgamation of men's and women's clothing including undergarments litter the hard wood floors. War finally achieved orgasm unloading deep in one of the women's wombs who's exactly he couldn't tell. He had become drunk off lust and at this point he'd cycled between the three of them.

After the amazing sensation of busting passed he shoved the three of them off of him and rolled out of bed hitting the floor with a wet thud. There on the cold wood surface he discovered a half empty bottle of liquor that he hungrily finished off, burped, farted and peeled himself from his resting place stumbling to the bathroom.

Over an hour later War escorted his lovely co-eds down the stairs through the foyer and out the front door, thanking them for the wonderful evening and making false promises of reconnecting again soon.

Just as soon as those women left the driveway, they would no longer exist to him. War's charming smile dissolved the second the door closed.

He was met by Will in the kitchen who was sitting at the center island, casually sipping from a freshly blended fruit smoothie. War walked past and shook up his brother. Will shrugged him off and slid a large empty red mug over to him.

"Hey, the redhead said you were handsome, duh right, really??" War said, making a derisive gesture as he picked up the Vitamix blender and poured the smoothie mix into his cup. "She was definitely your type, bro."

"Yea, slutty, that's my type," Will said sarcastically in between sips of his fruit drink. "Hope you still got some energy, today's gonna be a long one."

War downed his drink in a few gulps and wiped his mouth with the back of his hand. "Brother, don't worry about me. I have plenty of energy. PLENTY, trust me."

He scooted in close to his brother and embraced him in a bear hug as he dry humped Will's leg like a dog in heat. The two rumbled playfully for a few minutes before coming to a draw. It was time to get ready and their morning routine was strenuous.

First order of business: Two hours of intense weight- lifting, cardio and plyometrics. You have to be fit and in tip top shape; as the job demands the best of you at all times, at any time. Afterwards they showered and got dressed. The weather in this part of the country is always a constant 80 degrees or higher with low humidity so it makes dressing for the day simple.

The pair headed to the garage but stopped at a door just before you reached the garage entryway. The door leads to a storage unit that houses a lethal secret. On the left side of the door there is a digital panel embedded in the wall. Once the code is inputted, the false wall slides to the side revealing a heavy-duty reinforced steel door. The entrance leads to an armory that doubles as a panic room/bunker in the event of a home invasion.

The room is nothing short of impressive. Wall to wall, the space houses every kind of firearm and munition. From small caliber derringer pistols to 40mm grenade launchers, a true gun enthusiast's dream. The twins both selected a pistol and corresponding magazines, a pocketknife, and War with his spicy personality grabbed an H.E grenade for good measure. Because every tactical arms man knows to account for the unexpected. Will gave him a judgmental side eye glance but then continued stuffing mags in the magazine pouch attached to his belt loop.

The rest of their supplies were previously loaded in duffle bags in the trunk of the vehicle they intended to drive today.

The garage door closes as they speed off down the windy road towards the city limits.

Chapter 2
Routine Visits

First stop

A visit to a reputable and reliable 'off the books' weapons dealer. Krasnyy, a seedy looking man with a thick accent, thinning combover hairstyle, reminiscent of 1930's mobsters, and a crooked smile. Probably the results of a lifetime of bare-knuckle brawls in his prime years. The dealer originated from somewhere in or near Russia before the fall of the USSR and was probably a war criminal or on someone's most wanted list. Confidentiality in this line of work is almost as valuable as the smooth functioning actions of a chrome lined bolt carrier group on a short piston stroke gas system mated with a Geissele trigger group.

The twins needed to refresh their inventory. Business has been good this season and, in this city, Krasnyy was the go to. New shipments of products are coming in on a continuous basis, some familiar hardware, while others are still in the development phases or military trials. These products should never see action in civil situations yet somehow Krasnyy has his hands on them.

Another lesson to learn in this line of work is don't ask questions that you literally can't live with the answers given. Products and money exchanges are never in same day transactions, an added layer of safety for both parties. Contrary to popular belief there is honor among thieves. Because misinterpreted disrespect could lead one or their loved ones to an early grave.

Once an agreement of products and quantity is reached, the pickup point is later determined. That's how Krasnyy operates, and the twins respect it. It's like an instacart for the shooter's world.

Second stop

The duo makes a scheduled stop at an office building in the center of Metro Downtown. Law offices, state commissioners, bank headquarters and financial advisors call this five-block radius home. To Will, this section of town always smelled like money. Like, there is the literal scent of freshly printed money wafting in the air. At the front desk, War blatantly flirted with the new cute young woman with the doe eyes, shoulder length hair and perfect titties, which applied a noticeable amount of pressure on the plastic buttons struggling to hold back her bountiful bosom yearning to be released from the blouse that is caging them.

She smells like some kind of sweet nectar like flower and the raw animalistic scent of pheromones that a woman releases when in the presence of a man that she would absolutely reproduce with. That atomic concoction is driving War crazy. He really is like a pitbull with the pink thing hanging out. It's not even a question of whether he will find his way into the young ladies pants or lack thereof but more so a question of when. A smart man and a betting man would say within 24 hours. He moves fast.

After War secured her phone number, the twins were met in the lobby by Greg Brauma, 'The Broker'. A stylish older man who owns the building. He also has multiple programs going on internally within the building but the business involving the twins is one he personally handles. He's taken a liking to them in a fatherly kind of way. That's if the fatherly type was one who spent thousands of dollars nightly on expensive hookers, high quality cocaine and brokering contract killings for various clientele; up to and including members of the United States government from time to time.

If you haven't put two and two together yet, the Love brothers are assassins, assets, mercenaries, hitmen, guns-for-hire…you get it. They have been for quite some time adequately trained in their prospective backgrounds. Both men joined different branches of the military on their 18th birthday.

War is an 8-year Marine veteran, Staff Sergeant scout sniper as well as a highly decorated member of MARSOC. He has multiple deployments and combat engagements in hot zones comprising various countries in the Middle East, and countries bordering Russia and Southern Asia.

Will is an 8-year veteran of the United States Navy. Also, a decorated E-8 Master Sergeant and member of Seal Team 5 with deployments and engagements in the Middle East, various countries in South America and numerous countries on the east and northern coast of Africa.

The ranks of each brother don't seem to add up to their age and time served. The reason why they achieved such amazing feats was their hyper competitive nature between each other. No one outside of their world really existed to them; it was always those two against each other and eventually that morphed into them against the world. After what they had witnessed in their lifetime; the carnage, the greed, the need to kill people, because for some justice wasn't blind, she'd been instructed to turn the other way for one reason or another. When that happens, the need arises for an entity outside of law and order to correct the balance. And they were that corrective action! After they completed their second terms of military service, the twins decided it was time for a career change.

The brothers heard about the private sector; a range of motion with limited restraints and were all in. Early on they operated as private security for high-ranking personnel, traveling the world for the next three and a half years. While on a protection detail assignment to safeguard citizens of a small township in a 3rd world country in Southwestern Africa, they were approached by Brauma who at the time was a CIA liaison. Brauma had heard and seen footage of things those boys were capable of with just some 556 ammo, a couple of pineapple grenades, some time and a whole hell of a lot of nuts. Which brings us to the present day.

Brauma's office is reminiscent of mob bosses. Black marble and gold trimming were everywhere. His office had a perfectly unobstructed view of the city and the lingering sweet scent of $1000 cigars of which he puffed regularly, greeting them as they entered the gargantuan office space. Brauma ushered the men to their seats and took a seat behind his desk. A 70 inch television on the wall was displaying a news reporter's story about growing tensions between warring countries in the Middle East. The reporter said she feared that things would escalate and there would be many casualties in the future as the result of it.

"Nations will rise against nations, and kingdoms against kingdoms," Brauma stated, shaking his head sadly.

"Gentlemen, gentlemen. My two favorite guys," clapping his hands once shifting attention to the matter at hand. "Hey let me get you fellas a drink. War, I know you! You're like me, you want a double shot of the good stuff?"

War smiled and shot him the cowboy finger salute.

"And Will, the health nut right? Water? Coffee?" Will gestured for the water. A few minutes later a drop dead gorgeous redhead in a business skirt too short and several sizes too small to be legal for work, waltzed in with a serving tray with War and Brauma's drinks neat in tumblers and Will's icy bottle of water. War made googly eyes at her totally disregarding the ongoing business conversation. That is until Will smacked him on the back of the head.

Brauma laughs heartily, "I swear you guys are the sons I never had. Listen, here's the file on your next target. He is a prominent official on the Board of National Affairs for the government of Saudi Arabia and a Saudi oil prince. He's making waves reconfiguring petroleum prices to his liking.. price gouging. Saudi fucks! He's operating without consulting the American and U.N council. The Elitist aren't willing to tolerate this. The client wants him taken off the board. They want it loud and messy to send a clear and concise message to his constituents."

The target will be in Monaco, France in 72 hours for a planned business meeting with private interest. You two will arrive in France in 24 hours. You'll be given copies of potential routes he is going to take and the location of the Saudi Embassy he will be residing at during his stay. The how and the when are completely up to you. The fee is $500 large, half now and half after the jobs are done. You know how it goes. Any questions?"

"Yea, one. Is the redhead available?" War said, glancing at the closed office door.

Will just shook his head. Brauma laughed and toasted his drink with them.

With business agendas satisfied for the day the brothers set off to indulge in recreational activities to relax them before they left for the next mission. War recruited a flock of women to help ease his mind and body while Will decided he would take a relaxing motorcycle ride around the city. Will grabbed his helmet and on the way out his brother surfaced from his whore tsunami to poke fun at his brother's hidden purpose for his relaxing ride.

"Bro….Tell your little coffee chick I said hello!"

Will shook his head before walking out. The 1000 cc race track inspired motorcycle angrily roared to life and in two shifts of the gears he was gone in less than 60 seconds, nothing more than the faded spooling up of the motor and signature of the obnoxiously loud exhaust until he was out of ear shot. Will took this time to free his mind and let the road lead him wherever but most times it always led him to the same location. A nice little cafe on the far side of town away from the chaos of fast cars and loose women. But admittedly it was never the coffee or the croissants that drew him here. It was a specific employee, a barista. She was captivating. Chocolatey smooth skin that looked buttery from the touch. A short curly haircut framing her adorably innocent looking face, a million dollar smile and an angel's laugh. Will was sure that if his career afforded him the luxury of falling in love with someone, and not being overly concerned with a threat discovering his identity and in turn violently murdering his love interest in some sadistic form of revenge, it would be her he would love.

He frequented this cafe enough to where she remembered him whenever he came in. She knew his order before even he placed it. They would chat for a while and then he would get his drink, finish it and leave.

Occasionally she would step away from the counter to wipe tables down when business was slow. More of an excuse to converse with Will rather than the need to go above and beyond as an outstanding employee. She had no idea he was in love with her and as far as he was concerned, she never would. It was just safer for her that way.

Will returned home to the usual host of auditory sounds. Loud music and the sound of several women engaging in group sex was emanating from behind the doors leading to War's room. Will exhaustedly trekked to his room and shut the door.

Chapter 3
All In a Day's Work

15 hours later the brothers' plane is preparing to land on the airstrip in Monaco, France. It's a comfortable 78 degrees and a light breeze is blowing from the east. A car is awaiting their arrival on the tarmac. They toss the driver their bags and hop in.

Once they are at their hotel, they waste no time getting to work. The next day is chopped up into segments of counter surveillance and prep work. Hitting the target at the Embassy is a no go. Security is tight. They do explosive sweeps on vehicles entering and exiting the premises. With multiple checkpoints and armed guards, a hit behind the gates would cause way too many issues for them and probably resulted in their deaths. So, they mapped out the Saudi prince's route and devised a plan.

70 hours into the mission...

The Love brothers were sitting on the street side, second floor of an outdoor restaurant enjoying brunch. "Is the weather always this nice?" War asked, leaning back in his seat, shifting his sunglasses on his face.

Will shrugged, it was very rare that they had the opportunity to enjoy the scenery while on missions so he was taking full advantage of the time, even occasionally daydreaming about him and the barista girl, holding hands strolling down Main Street and staring in through the shop windows, like normal people. War made a declaration that he would have to add this destination to his list of stops once he retired from the business, mentioning also that he bet the women there were freaks in the bedroom as he ordered another coffee while they waited for their meals to arrive.

An hour into brunch they had somehow gotten on the subject of Will's love life or lack thereof and brought up the barista at the cafe. Will wasn't the nervous type but speaking about her caused a visual shift in him that his brother quickly noticed.

"Oh, wow bro! You really like this girl huh? Not the I wanna fuck you silly like. But the I want the white picket fence, the kids, the dog, the minivan type of like."

Will laughed at the ridiculousness of his brother's comment. The simple fact was that he was amazed because it was a concept, he was willing to entertain...

War said, "Look, all I'm saying is there is no time like the present. If you're digging her like that, say something. What's the worst that could happen? She's not gonna say no or turn you down bro, you were blessed with my looks!"

Will rolled his eyes. "Right. Because once I tell her, 'Hey yea I think I love you. I dream of running away and starting a family with you. But oh wait before I do that let me inform you that I'm a paid American Asset. I kill people for a living and my life is in a constant state of danger oh on average 90% of the time. I'll probably never be able to fully relax around you because I've killed people in almost every country and I'm sure that karma is gonna come back to haunt me one day. But if you can get past that, this is a pretty sweet deal...'"

War laughed loud and hearty. "Bro! Exactly. That's what I tell these women and it's guaranteed to get you laid. Trust me!"

Will snickered and shook his head. "Where are we on time?"

War looked at a device sitting on the table that resembled a tablet. He activated it and an image appeared on the screen was a map of the city and a red blip. They were tracking the Saudi via a tracking device they attached to his vehicle days ago while trailing the target.

"Making good time. ETA 18 minutes until they

cross the grid," War said.

The brothers chatted for a bit longer. The tablet chimed letting them know the target was 7 minutes out. Will asked for the check and paid for their meal. War left a handsome tip for the waiter and they hurried to the stairs.

"5 minutes out."

Once they were on the street, Will glanced past War's shoulder off in the distance to see if he could visually spot the target vehicle but there was no sign of it yet. The street they were sitting on was a straight away with a few traffic signals breaking up the monolithic strip of road. Minutes later War spotted the marked black luxury sedan turning the corner and he nodded to his brother.

Will acknowledged, "Visual of the target vehicle confirmed. Arming charges."

He pulled out his phone, switching to an app that displayed the word 'Disarmed' and a button on a blue screen. Once he armed it the screen turned red and displayed the word 'Armed'. They walked out past another shop entrance doors just as the Saudi Prince's transport vehicle was passing by. The street they were on was a two-lane roadway with multi- level brick buildings lining the sidewalks. Vehicles were parked bumper to bumper along the roadway, packed tightly like sardines in a can.

The trigger planted on the target vehicle was a simple red light laser beacon inserted in the grill of the vehicle via a well- placed sniper shot courtesy of War. This location had been pre-prepped and designated as the attack zone because of the limited mobility, density of vehicles and suspected ongoing road construction that would force traffic down this corridor.

There was a digital road sign that indicated if the lanes were opened or closed. Will had hacked the system earlier that day and when the target vehicle was in sight, he manually switched the signs indicating the lanes were closed except for the lane they needed open, funneling the target right down the street they occupied. Will had secretly attached six 2 pound forward facing explosives claymores to six individual vehicles in a box shape configuration that covered both sides of the street. The target vehicle would drive into the configuration unaware of the dangers and once the red laser beacon broke the plane of the laser light attached to the explosives it would detonate all 36 small charges simultaneously, engulfing the vehicle in a wave of 2-inch diameter metallic ball bearings with an accompanying fireball.

"BAAAAAAMMM!!"

The explosion rocked the streets setting off cars and building alarms for blocks and shattered windows of store fronts. The blast was contained within the kill box, and no one was seriously injured beyond its perimeter.

Will watched as the car fire blazed for a moment before taking out his phone and dialing a number.

"It's done…"

He ended the call and he and his brother strolled off picking back up on their conversation prior.

A week later Will was home, feet propped up on the couch catching up on some reading material when he received a pinged message to his phone. It was Brauma. He was scheduling a meeting for a couple of hours from now. Will hollered from the steps to War checking to see if he'd received the same message. He did. A little while later the brothers arrive at the office where Brauma is elated to see them.

"Guys! My guys! We need to have a toast! You did it! You two fucking guys did it! We're in the big leagues now boys!

Will and War had no idea what he was talking about but they were pleased, that was for sure. Brauma continued excitedly, "We acquired a new client who just contacted me. This is one of those big fish in the pond, the kind your uncle's friend used to brag about catching. The unicorn. They were very impressed with your tactics, boys. Another important mission! They want to meet us in person. This is great news!

"When?", War asked.

Brauma shrugged, "No clue."

Will and War exchange looks.

"Where?", Will questioned.

"Also, I don't know. They'll contact us. You know these types are…"

Chapter 4
When You Meet the Boogey Man

Months later

The three of them are on a black stinger
helicopter enroute to the location of a yacht sailing in the
Indian Ocean. Salty water whips up from the blue ocean
surface as the helicopter circles before landing on the sea
vessel's landing port. The vessel was enormous. From
overhead it's easily 40 yards long. More like a cruise
liner than a personal vehicle, heavily guarded too.
Guards greeted and guided the men from the helipad out
of the wake of the rotors wash. Once on board, War,
Will and Brauma are patted down, their weapons
removed and stored before allowed entry beyond the
landing port.

The interior of the yacht was stunning. The
whole thing was like a floating castle. They were led
down a hallway to a room filled with windows that
allowed the sun to shine through from all angles, that
made Will feel strangely like a fish in a bowl.

The room is sea level with a staircase heading up to the deck above the ocean's surface. A Caucasian male, older, solidly built and ruggedly tough looking, refined like a war hardened veteran, was sitting on a fancy white couch that wrapped around the length of the lower deck. He was clipping the end of a cigar when the trio was brought to him. He motioned for the gentlemen to have a seat. They sat there in silence as this gentleman clipped, lit and enjoyed a lengthy puff from his cigar. A guard brought the host a laptop and set it down on the glass coffee table that was between them.

At this point the host still hadn't uttered one word and just kept jetting his eyes back and forth between the three of them while puffing his cigar. Brauma caught movement out of his peripheral. His subtle but noticed movement caused the Love brothers to look in the same direction. They all caught sight of an amazing grace of a woman gliding onto the deck, the sunbathing her perfectly sculpted body in golden rays.

She was tall, olive coloured with honey yellow eyes. Full succulent lips. Jet black hair flowing down her back that ever so gently swept across the top of her round ass. She's wearing a 2 piece and a tasteful coverup to conceal her magnificent physique, but the fabric was failing at its task horribly. She breezed by the men and found a comfortable spot on the couch nestling beside the host and produced a USB drive from somewhere on her person. She locked eyes with War and held his gaze just long enough for him to feel the temperature rise in his pants before she broke the link and slid the USB into the laptop. She keyed in a command and pushed the device into the center of the table and sat back. Finally, the host spoke.

"This is Teagan Butterum. Former NSA analyst. He extracted valuable data from a secure network at a military installation in Guam and when discovered he fled out of the country. Recovery of deleted files on his personnel desktop yielded evidence of possible collusion with foreign entities. Entities that view the American government as the enemy and not a valuable ally. We believe he's planning on selling the pirated data on the black market and this intel will directly compromise the integrity of America's infrastructure. This cannot happen."

"Any intel on a last known location?" Brauma asked.

Mr. Nobody, the host, replied, "Last known location was a villa in Los Ladrillos, Panama."

War questioned, "An American?"

"Yes...."

Next was Will, "Any other viable intel? Security details? Sec ops?"

The scantily clad woman, Mrs. Nobody, shifted and then answered, "As of right now he has refuge and backing from a Panamanian Military General."

"What's our window?"

Mr. Nobody, "The trade will happen in the next couple of days. The deal is not to go through. Retrieve the data and hand deliver it to me."

Brauma questioned, "And the target, eliminated I presume?"

"Your presumption is correct," Mr. Nobody said, lighting his cigar again. My associates want him extinguished."

Will spoke this time, "We'll need time to gather further pertinent intel to ensure mission positive success."

Here Mrs. Nobody looked at the team with disdain. "I thought you were the best they had to offer? Efficient and able to work with limited resources, were our associates wrong?"

War gives an egotistical smile and says, "Sweety, we are the best your money can buy. The job isn't the difficult part. I can put a bullet in a target over a mile away, while scratching my nuts with one hand and trust me that's no easy task. We need as much intel as possible to make our jobs that much easier. Who wants to break a sweat, unless it's for good reason of course..."

Mr. Nobody glanced at War with his emotionless eyes as Mrs. Nobody smirked at War's brazen remark. Mr. Nobody took notice of his mate's reactions. He drug his hand across Mrs. Nobody's buttery tanned thigh taking great care to drive his palm up and underneath her cover up in front of War intentionally.

"The job pays 3 million US currency. I will provide all the intel you need to achieve the objective. This needs to be taken care of as soon as possible. Success could spell out more opportunities in the future."

Mrs. Nobody unplugged the USB drive and handed it over to Brauma but War reached out and took it from
her, caressing her soft hand in the process. Brauma and Will winced at the sight of the unwarranted contact. Mr. Nobody however didn't react at all. He relit his cigar and sat back again.

"Contact me when the mission is complete. My men will escort you back to your helicopter now.

And just like that the meeting was adjourned. Brauma put his shades on and excused himself. The Love brothers did the same. Mr. Nobody's guards handed them their weapons back once they were on the landing pad and stood on guard until the chopper was airborne. The ride was silent for a while, only the sounds of the engines overhead as the craft cut through the air as it headed back to shore. Brauma was the first to speak.

"War, you got a serious set on you!"

Laughter erupted and all, but Will laughed.

He knew his brother's weakness for beautiful women and his reckless nature could potentially become dangerous for them. He chose at that moment to say nothing and ruin the mood since nothing came of it but when they were alone, he would address it with War then. For now, Will's mind was elsewhere.

Chapter 5
Introductions Are In Order

Days later

Will had gone on another spirited run on his motorcycle that night. The intent was to give his brother room to clear his head the way he clears it and it's giving Will a chance to clear his. There was an event down at the oceanfront where thousands of beachgoers crowded the strip. Will traveled several blocks west of the parties and found a quiet spot on the beach.

There was a solitary wooden bench that lined the walkway right where the sand meshed with the last bit of the concrete. Will pulled up and shut his bike off. The sound of the ocean waves breaking on the shore was therapeutic. There was a beach house fifteen feet down from where he sat. He could tell from the music and sea of bodies that they were having a party. The intoxicating scent from the grill made its way to that lonely bench and the aromas made his mouth water and his stomach grumble. He began to think about it. A simple house party. A gathering of friends. Something that he's never attended. From childhood he and his brother didn't have the best conditions growing up and then straight from high school to the military.

The commotion and laughter resonating from the house made him smile to himself. He just sat there for hours, quietly admiring the festivities.

A group of women had migrated to the back patio and were drinking and talking pretty loudly for that time of night when one of them looked over the railing toward Will. The lady was familiar. It took a few minutes for it to sink in but when he realized who she was, he sat up. It was the barista from the cafe. To think, he has been going to her cafe for over a year and still did not know her name. After a while some of the girls decided to take the party to the beach and undressed down to bikinis for some and panties and a bra for the others.

That was Will's que to head out. He didn't want to feel like a creep for watching these vixens prancing about. He stood up to head back to his motorcycle when he heard a sweet voice calling to him from behind.

He turned and it was his coffee mate jogging up the ramp to him. Her eyes were lit up even in the night sky.

"Hey you! You're down here for the party?"

"Huh, no," Will said awkwardly. "I took a ride

earlier and found myself down here. Was taking in the sights. I wasn't staring or anything…"

She smiled, "It's ok if you were. The party is kind of lame. Hey, I realized as much as we see each other I don't know your name...?

"William. My friends call me Will."

"Will? Ok Will, can I call you that?" He nodded.

"Cool. I'm Stella." reaching out a hand. "Now we have been formally introduced."
A twinkle came to her eyes from the ones in the sky. Will warmed up a bit.

"Stella…it's cute. It fits."

"Yea I know it sounds like an old woman's name. It was my mother's. It's Latin, it means…"

"Star …" Will said. Looking like he fell in love at that moment.

"Yes! Most people don't know that!"

They smiled shyly at each other for a few seconds then Stella made a comment about his motorcycle. She'd never ridden on one. Will told her the specs on his bike, taking note not to brag about the price. It was distasteful and he wanted the girl to like him for him and not for his bank account.

Her friends tried to get her to join them in the water, but she declined. She told them she had other plans, she was taking a nighttime ride with her friend and turned to face Will who hesitated before agreeing.

She ran back to the house to change into something more appropriate for a ride then returned in minutes. Will fastened an extra helmet he had on her pretty little head, making sure to be extra gentle pushing the curls out of her face then showed her how to get on the vehicle, how and where to place her hands around him. She squeezed tighter than expected but he didn't mind it. Through his helmet he could smell the perfume she wore and it was a cloud of pure bliss. Warm vanilla and sugar. The bike roared to life and like that they were a blur.

Hours later they were sitting at a late-night diner enjoying a meal and each other's company. The laughs were plentiful between bites of food. He learned all he could about her; she learned what he wanted her to know about himself. He couldn't fully emerge her into his world just yet. That wouldn't be safe for either of them right now. But to feel human, normal. Like an everyday person. That was reward enough for Will and he chose to relish every second of this normality.

His brother's voice continuously echoed in the back of his mind taunting him with what the benefits were of telling her his profession, but he shook that dumb idea off. Things were going better than he could've ever planned, that is until a few drunk fellas stumbled into the diner being annoying and obnoxious. They sat at the bar directed across from Will and Stella. One of the guys must've noticed how attractive Stella was because he tapped the other guy's shoulder, and they looked back at Will and her a few times. Will noticed and tried to pay the guys no mind and continue his date until one of them interrupted.

"Hey, buddy. I see you gotta helmet...Is that your bike out there? Nice..." his voice wanders off. "Hey, you hear me talking to you!"

Will turned and smiled calmly and responded with a simple head nod and a thank you. One of the other drunk guys thumbed it up but the belligerent one insulted Will and his bike. Will guessed it was because he didn't respond in a quick enough fashion.

He paid the asshole no mind and continued talking to his date. The drunkard didn't like that he was being ignored and decided to escalate the matter. Will would've stayed cool if he had not noticed that Stella's breathing changed from slow and steady to ragged. Her eyes shifted nervously, constantly from him to that group behind them. It was visible she was becoming uneasy now.

"Stella, it's ok. Are you ready to leave?"

She looked at Will then at the group of men and nodded her head. Will slid from out of the booth seat, stretching his hand to help Stella to her feet and politely excused himself and his date hoping that the men would backoff. His excusing them only stoked the flames. One of the men leapt from his barstool and placed a grubby paw on his shoulder and that was it. Will gestured with a subtle tip of his head and a hand motion to Stella to hold on for a minute and if she would back up a few steps. She had no idea what he was doing but for some reason the look on his face brought a measure of ease to her troubled spirit.

She complied and when she was out of range, he turned to face the 'gentlemen'.

"Look, we don't want any trouble. I see and can smell that you boys have been in the good stuff. I know liquor alters one's thoughts and actions and I'm not putting you at fault for that. We just want to go peacefully. That's all."

Drunk guy number one balled his fist up telegraphing his intention and launched a sloppy left hook that Will saw coming a mile away. He effortlessly slipped the poorly structured blow and returned a calculated throat punch to drunk guy number one that sent him to his knees gasping for air like a fish out of water. Drunk guy two ran up but received a kick to the ankle that bent the joint at a 90 degree angle snapping tendons and shattering the bone like when you smash a fluorescent light bulb and followed up with a swift elbow to the jaw line which cracked the hinge on one side of his face and laid him on his back on the diners sticky floor. Drunk guy number three saw how easily his buddies were disabled and hesitated wondering if he would meet the same painful fate.

Will shifted his head left to right, cracking his

neck in expectation of the coming fight and raised his fist in a defense stance. He motioned for the drunkard to bring it on and that was all it took. Drunk guy three ran out of the establishment bailing on his comrades with his tail between his legs. A smart move on his part. When Will turned around Stella's eyes were as big as saucer plates. They almost matched the size of the smile plastered across her fat cheeks.

"Whoa! Where'd you learn that?" she asked excitedly.

"Uh...took a few lessons at the Y."

He nervously laughed as he fished through his pockets and left the payment for the food and a hefty tip on the counter along with an apology. The waitress graciously thanked him and went back to her duties but not before informing the line cook to call the ambulance for the guys knocked out on the floor.

A little while later Will was pulling up in front of Stella's house. He shut his bike down and gingerly pulled her helmet off. That almost comically large smile was still visible on her face. She stood staring at him as if she were waiting for something, perhaps a dream to come true.

"Well, I really enjoyed tonight," she said softly.

"Yea, sorry about the diner. I wasn't gonna hurt 'em but I thought they may have tried to hurt you and I want you to always feel safe around me. So, I had..."

As he spoke, she leaned in and planted a soft slow kiss on his lips ceasing his speech mid-sentence. Her lips were warm. Moist but not too much, just enough to raise the temperature around them. He wrapped his arms around her waist and she let him draw her in.

"Well…," clearing his throat, "Can I call you?"

She hurriedly typed her number into his phone then kissed him again and strolled towards the gates leading up to her front door, beaming the whole way. Will waited until she

vanished beyond her apartment doors before, he put his helmet back on concealing a smile of his own.

The next morning Will was woken up to the pleasing aroma of robust coffee yanking him from the dream world. War was waving a cup back and forth below his nostrils. The games never cease with this one.

"Wakey wakey eggs and bakey! Hello, Sunshine! You've spent the last hour smiling in your sleep. Must've had a good night. Wake up, put some clothes on! We got a conference call with Brauma. It's go time!"

[During the Conference call]

"Gentlemen! We have a visual of the target via satellite confirmation. Mr. Nobody's intel was accurate. Mr. Butterum is residing at a villa in the hills, secluded and heavily guarded by Panamanian military forces as

36

previously mentioned. We think he's preparing to make a move so our window of opportunity will be a short one. Now, I'm not going to bullshit you, this is gonna be one for the books. The probability of survival is slim. I'll provide overwatch from drone surveillance and everything that I can from my end and coordinate with my contacts for an extraction point. You'll need to recover the hard copy data. It's stored in a safe in the target's room, bedside, right of the doorway. It was requested that the target be eliminated as well and to make it quick and clean. All stipulations must be met in order for payment to be rendered and boys I want my 15 percent! You'll arrive by seaplane in 18 hours. Let's get her done! Whatever gear and weapons you need will be provided to you in flight. Good luck fellas even though I know you won't need it. Heads on a swivel. I'm proud to know you all, just felt compelled to say that."

Phone goes dead.

Chapter 6
Mission Possible

18 hours later the little white plane coasted over the ocean surface, slashing the waves and eventually sloshing to a stop just off the shoreline. Seagulls cawed overhead and the smell of briny water reinvigorated the brothers as they exited the craft.

A boat was awaiting them on their arrival. The Love brothers carried duffle bags with loadouts specific to their unique talents. During the flight they were briefed on final mission plans and devised a plan of assault. War would provide overwatch from a perch in the hill side while Will would infiltrate and locate the target. They decided nighttime intel would best serve them.

The operation was to activate at 0300 hours. The brothers arrived and set off into the jungles surrounding the Destination resort.

[0245]

The Jungles of South America at night can be a scary place. Everything in this part of the world wants to kill you or kill and then eat you. A normal person would be petrified of the idea of sleeping in such a harsh environment but not the Love brothers. This is the stuff they live for.

"Wake up, sunshine! It's almost time to put in work!" Will said, nudging War's shoulder.

"I wasn't sleeping! I actually never sleep, bro. Ever. I don't know, maybe something's wrong with me. Or wrong with everybody else... yea I'ma go with that. You're actually butting in on a very rewarding scene from Bubble Butt Snatchers 3."

Will shook his head and rolled his eyes. Only his brother would be so bold as to be watching porn at a time like this. "Alrighty, think you could put your dick away just until we complete the mission?"

"Sorry big brother, I can't make any promises. I rock out with my cock out bro, you know the motto!"

They chuckled as Will crept down the hill side under the cover of darkness almost invisible. He moved between the trees and bushes finding a safe spot to stop and observe the area before keying into his brother's earbud.

"What's it looking like down range?"

"A good fucking time that's what! The target has been in his room since we arrived. He's eating, looks like burritos. Maybe chicken. Salsa."
Will coughed to interrupt his brother's shenanigans. "Right. There are two armed guards outside his room door. Three more patrolling the downstairs area. There are four guards patrolling the premises on continuous rotations. A sleeper guard is sitting in a higher up suite overlooking the targets, I'm assuming a sniper. By their posture I assume the guards are military, so once the first shot is fired this will be considered an international incident if we're captured. So, no mistakes."

Will shifted in anticipation, "Yep, let's wrap this up quickly then. I'm Oscar mike."

"Copy …. One to the head," said War.

"One to the heart," Will replied.
A motto the brothers have recited to each other sense their early military days.

War popped off a series of silenced headshots clearing a path for Will who was putting in some CQB work of his own, rifle against the guards that weren't in War's line of sight. Will took a moment to plant a small detonator and charge before continuing his path. During War's onslaught, one of the guards went down but had a nerve induced twitch resulting in him pulling the trigger until he expired.

Thirty rounds in the dead of night are the equivalent of a fire alarm in these kinds of conditions.

40

The call to arms was made and shit immediately hit the fan. A soldier radioed it in, and additional military personnel were summoned to the area.

The target became startled at the onslaught of gunshots and raced to his bedroom door but a single shot from War's long barreled sniper rifle sent a round pacing down range. It punched through the drywall next to him causing the target to pivot off his step and dash for cover behind the bed. War's precision rifle fire turned the target's bedroom into a sequestered island.

Brauma's voice pierced the air via radio chatter. "Excuse me fellas I don't know what the hell is going on but you got about 9 minutes before Panama's finest is in your ass. Two heavy assault vehicles heading your way. Pick up the pace. Transport is secured and awaiting you at the Exfil...MOVE YOUR ASS!!"

Will stalked the steps leading to the villa placing lethal shots on targets when needed. He took cover behind a corner wall that led to the hall at the front entrance of the target zone. Peeking around the corner he confirmed it was clear before proceeding.

When he arrived at the target's front door he slipped in through an opening and tiptoed to the bedroom door. Turning the handle slightly revealed that the door was locked but the knob was equipped with a cheap brass bolt and the locking mechanism snapped when Will applied a donkey kick near the latch. The door barely budged. That's when Will realized the target barricaded himself in with the furniture in the room.

Over the radio War advised that the target had armed himself with a pistol and was hiding in the bathroom. War went back and forth between keeping an eye on the areas of the target's room that he could see and making sure no combatants flanked his brother from the hallways, while Will worked on clearing the door. It took a minute but Will pushed the clutter back and was in the room. War guided him directly to Butterum's location where Will prepped a flashbang and in one smooth motion kicked the door in and tossed in the explosive instantly blinding and disorienting Butterum. Will didn't hesitate to put slugs in Butterum. One in the chest and one in the head at close range as he begged for his life. He holstered his pistol and dragged the body over to the safe which had a fingerprint scanner.

Placing the dead man's palm on the digital screen granted him access. Will took everything he thought was relevant from the confines of the safe and stuffed them in his pack. He jumped out of the bedroom window, landing on the platform and was about to make a beeline for the jungle where War was still providing overwatch when a barrage of gunfire halted him in his tracks. A Panamanian military vehicle came skirting around the corner nearly tipping over as soldiers on foot positioned themselves between them and the attackers.

One of Will's det chargers went off, lighting up the night sky. The driver skidded to a halt. More soldiers filed out and onto the street. War took aim but Will reacted first. He let loose with his rifle. The timed shots were exact, as round after round found its mark. The bolt locked signifying the magazine was empty. Instead of reloading he switched to his sidearm and dropped the last three soldiers.

"C'mon, buttercup. That ass isn't gonna move itself! Your guardian angel is running out of ammo. Move it!"

Another military vehicle peeled around the corner. This one was a small pickup truck with a 25 mm machine gun bolted down to the bed of the truck. A gunner was standing behind the controls and when Will came into view, he pulled the trigger. Bullets stitched the grass right in front of him. It was War's turn to show out. He lined up his crosshairs with the bridge of the gunner's nose and fired. From that distance through the zoom in lens, the man's head looked comical as it exploded into red bits and chunks.

The body toppled over the truck beds railing, right on top of a few soldiers standing behind. They knelt for cover and started firing wildly in the direction the recent shot came from. Smoking spent shell casings somersaulted from the ejection port of War's rifle as he lined up more faces in his sights. Despite the mound of headless corpses piling up behind the truck, the soldier still scrambled and attempted to mount the machine gun.

War's voice, "Uh brother, I'm burning through

ammo here. You wanna do something about that technical or are we just gonna play around with these fuckers all night?"

"Yea yea... Hold your horses. I couldn't have all the fun or else you'd bitch about it the whole trip home." Will calmly remove a shell from his front pouch and slid it into the m203 launcher attached to his short barrel rifle and the moment he heard the report from War's weapon and saw another potential gunner drop he lined up the shot. Thump. The hollow sound of the large projectile filled his ears as it spiraled through the air and knocked a hole in the hood of the pickup truck a split second before the vehicle went up in a dazzling fire ball.

The concussion from the blast scattered the surrounding soldiers creating a window for Will to sprint to the tree line. War pumped a fist as he watched his brother take out multiple targets at once. Will was safely concealed in the underbrush when he radioed to War to pack it up and meet at the Exvil. Mission accomplished!

There was a single engine Cessna plane parked on the dirt runway. Will was an excellent pilot. War pulled security while Will cycled through the startup functions of the craft and in minutes the turbines were spooling up. The propels started spinning and that's when Will signaled to his brother to hop in.

The takeoff was rough due to the dirt road but in minutes they were airborne and headed back to the States. Once they were clear of the danger zone, War howled like a wild beast. Will mimicked his brother's actions howling in turn as they fist bumped. This one would definitely go down in the books.

24 hours later - Conference call with Mr. Nobody

"Nice work gentlemen, very nice. Things got interesting for a bit, but you pulled it off. National authorities have no idea who the assaulters were and currently no nation is claiming fault, excellent. Keep it up and you and your men will be able to retire. I'll be in contact soon with the next objective."

The screen went black.

Brauma was brimming with joy. The operation was a complete success and there was a three million dollar payout minus Brauma's 15% commission, of course. At the look of it there was plenty more work and much more money to be made.

Soon as the call ended Will was up and headed towards the exit. He had special plans tonight and even more reason to celebrate.

Chapter 7
All Good Things End

The seasons passed. Will and Stella's relationship was akin to the Middlemist Red. The rarest flower in the world, in that it only blooms in two locations and there is only one of each specimen. Their relationship turned into a thing that he never thought he would ever obtain in this lifetime.

She was the first thing he thought about when he woke up and usually the last thing that crossed his mind before he closed his eyes at night. He looked forward to her calls and kisses. He studied her routine, became familiar with her love language and spoke it fluently. He knew her habits and her tics like they were his own. When she would become stressed, he knew that coffee was one thing that cut the tension. He was the other major source of her stress relief.

Countless times Will would find himself

daydreaming about her in between gunshots and explosions. Devising plans for their future while devising plans for escape or evade scenarios. She was changing him, and he was boosting her confidence.

The shy timid girl he met at that coffee shop all those years ago was blossoming into a bold woman and he adored her. When he would return after a mission, she would greet him at the door of her apartment wearing that angelic smile and usually little to nothing else, which never ceased to amaze him. Oftentimes they rarely made it to her bedroom during the first session.

Work was going outstandingly well. The money flowed steadily like a river into the brothers' accounts. Life was good, in fact too good.

Mr. Nobody has never met at the same location twice. Who knows if it's in part of his paranoia or the fact that he's a busy man either way it made face to face meetings interesting. Sometimes he was accompanied by Mrs. Nobody, other times it was just him and occasionally when he was too busy with other affairs, he sent her to delegate on his behalf.

Just dealing with her made Will and Brauma uneasy. War on the other hand was delighted with those 'just her' encounters, for personal reasons of course. It was obvious he was enthralled with her physically and she was surely intrigued with him. Playing with fire, that was War's modus operandi.

War pulled into a parking structure and drove to the top deck. He parked his car in the same row as an SUV. They were the only two vehicles in attendance on that level. He stepped out of his vehicle and casually strolled to the back end of the truck where the door was ajar. He slid in and found Mrs. Nobody sitting snuggled up on the far side of the bench seats, looking seductive in a matching bra and panties set, red bottom heels. She was draped in a thick plush fur coat that appeared almost as soft as she was. It swaddled her like she was a newborn baby, concealing a tasteful surprise for her boy toy beneath. She held wine glasses in one hand and a bottle of expensive vino in the other.

Once the door was closed, she set the bottle and the wine glasses down and crawled over to him on her hands and knees like a lioness stalking its prey. When she reached him she unbuckled his pants, removed his pistol, tossing it to the floor haphazardly and in one motion pulled down his pants and boxer briefs down. Grabbing onto his manhood in one hand she swallowed him whole, all the way to the balls while maintaining eye contact. She knew War loved that type of aggressive act. That sent flares of pleasure rushing through his body. He wrapped a handful of her long flowing coal colored hair in his fist and forced more of himself down her throat which she gladly welcomed. Saliva, like a geyser,

48

poured from her mouth as she let him have his way with her.

He had to stop her from bringing him to orgasm with her oral skills so instead of busting he grabbed her by her throat and rested her on the cushion of the bench seat. Pulling her thongs to the side he spread her lips. She was already juicy and her nectar drizzled down between her cheeks. His tongue found her clit and he began sucking, licking and spitting on her peach slice. She'd never been treated like this by any man before. It was assertive, domineering and passionate all at the same time. She wanted more and more of it. More of him. Usually, her status frightened men but not this one. War ravaged her like she was a common hooker that he met at a bar, taking delight in watching her shiver from repeated orgasms. Her breaths were short and she found herself panting like a dog in heat. Her phone buzzed. It was an incoming call from somebody whose number wasn't saved.

"You wanna answer that?" War said between muffled breaths.

She took her phone and flung it to the other side of the car. It clattered up against the dashboard before dropping from sight. She turned back to War and shoved his head back down between her legs. He continued feasting on her greedily.

Once he felt she reached her tipping point he flipped her over without warning and inserted himself in her from behind, burrowing deep. She exhaled in ecstasy as she orgasmed again. The SUV rocked rhythmically while the sexcapade went on for hours on end.

At the same time on another side of town slow jams played over the recessed speakers in the wall. Will embraced Stella's supple brown frame in his arms. Planting wet kisses on her lips and then on her neck making a pit stop at her ample breasts. He lingered there for a moment showing equal gratitude for each round brown mound and the adorning chocolate chip colored nipple atop it.

A light coat of perspiration layered her skin as he traveled further south. He lifted up her tiny body above his, resting her legs on his broad shoulders and buried his face in her pussy as she held onto his head for dear life suspended off the floor. He kept her there until she screamed and overflowed down his chin. Her juices poured out dribbling onto his chest like clear sticky strands of honey. She begged for him to come inside her and then and only then did he release her. Her legs were weak but she felt compelled to reciprocate. She pushed Will back on the bed and little by little she explored his body. She held her breath and swallowed as much of his member as she could. Will yelped at the sensations which drove her wild. When it was time for him to feel her interior, she was soaking wet. They made love the whole night; their appetites never fully satiated until they eventually passed out.

Will woke up a little while later and she was curled up in his arms. The moonlight streamed in with a soft glow that made her look like a chocolate angel laying beside him. He kissed her forehead lightly and stroked her back. Instinctively, she nestled in closer to him and sighed a sound of relief in her sleep that was strangely pleasing to his soul. He was content with her. Nothing mattered more. The money. The missions. He even lingered on the thoughts of his and his brother's relationship. For the longest time it was those two against the world and now his world was changing. This was all new, frightening and yet so appealing. He was hooked, line and sinker. He thought to himself, "I can do this forever."

The months roll by, and Will and Stella's relationship continues to grow, nearly spending every day together when he's not away on business. She still had no idea what he did for a living and what little details he provided led to him being a broker of sorts.

It explained the frequent business trips and expendable assets at his disposal. How else could he afford such an expensive lifestyle? One evening they were relaxing in the tub he was reclining up against her body, rubbing her feet as she sang to him and stroked his hair while tracing soapy hearts across his chest. Her voice was melodic and soothing. Mesmerizing, like a siren's song, almost rocking him to sleep when he heard her speak just above a whisper.

"I could do this forever…."

Will simpered as she kissed him on the cheek. "Me too!"

Stella struggled with the words she didn't say out loud that she wanted to. The part where she declared she had fallen in love with him and wanted to marry him and spend forever together, but also because she missed her last two periods. She'd secretly taken a pregnancy test, several of them, and they all came up positive. She would tell him at the right time and place. Tonight, though, she chose to spend the time the way they were right at that moment.

One evening Will and War were out eating and carrying out surveillance on a target provided by Mr. Nobody, of course.

War spoke in the silence between bites of his sandwich. "So, little brother. You and the coffee chick… y'all are getting pretty serious, huh?"

"Stella! And yea bruh she is amazing. She's smart and beautiful. She's my peace. The noise in my head goes away when I'm with her. It's like everything else stops. I've never felt this feeling before!"

War said nothing, he just continued eating. Will continued, "I'm glad you brought her up. There's something I've been meaning to talk to you about. After this mission is done, I'm done. I'm out. I have a nice nest egg saved up, bro. I'm going to ask her to marry me. Get a house, the white picket fence and a swinging chair on the front porch. Get a dog and have a couple of little rugrats, you know…?" laughing to himself.

"Really?? You're gonna leave this? What about the work?? Taking down the shit birds of the world. What about Brauma? What about me and you! Double tap! The twin terrors! One to the head, one to the heart! You're going to give it all up for her??! She's worth that?"

"Yes! She is! It changes nothing between us. We'll still be brothers and Brauma will be just fine. You'll be just fine. Nothing changes, nothing."
War trying to hold the yell in, "Everything changes!"

Silence between them. Will takes a deep breath.

"Bro, I need this. We're getting older. Life at thirty-five isn't the same at twenty-five. Life is all about change. Staying in the same place, staying stagnant isn't natural. We were in totally different places when we started this journey all those years ago. I need for you to accept this. I'm leading point on this one and I need you to have my 6, bro."

War pushes all the tension and disagreement down in back of his mind. "I hear you. I see how you've changed. You can smell it. I'm happy for you. For yall, I guess. She's good for you, bro. After you get the house with the picket fence maybe I'll come and visit."

Will slapped his brother on the back in an endearing manner. His approval meant more to him than War could ever know, he knew his brother would be ok.

They share the same blood and that bond could never be broken. He had been thinking about his progression with Stella and the relationship with him and his brother for a long time. It was finally time for things to come to a head. He definitely did not want to split up their duo but a force stronger than he was pulling him in another direction. Will was in love, and it wasn't a doubt in his mind that he wanted to spend the rest of his life with Stella. He made the decision that night that in a couple of days when they returned home, he would pop the question.

Chapter 8
Let The Chips Fall Where They May

After precise planning, the pinpoint execution of the perfect date night was topped off by an amazing day of pampering Stella, which included an extravagant dinner at an exclusive rooftop restaurant and a carriage ride in the park. Will ended that portion of the evening on one knee, presenting a huge diamond ring to the love of his life in front of the whole world which consisted of a handful of couples walking and a few homeless people rummaging through the trash cans. Of course, she said yes and showered him with kisses.

Later, when it was announced at an intimate dinner function, Brauma called for a toast to congratulate Will. Will informed Brauma of his future retirement plans and the old man understood oh too well the supernatural powers a woman possessed over a man.

He gave Will a hug and kissed his fiancés on the cheek congratulating them both and wished them well.

Brauma had moves to make and was about to head out but stopped beside War who was hanging around in the entrance way of the dining room sipping on a glass of brown liquor.

"Your brother looks happy."

"Yea, that's what he says."

"Cheer up, bud, it's not that bad. It's not the end of the world. Now we only cut the profits two ways," Brauma chuckled.

"You gonna be ok?" he asked, sobering up.

War scoffed, "Fuck yea. I didn't voluntarily end my life. He did." Sarcastically laughs while taking another sip of his cup of misery.

Brauma shakes his head. "I'm heading out. Got some new accounts for you at the top of next week. Things might change up a little bit but we'll adapt. Call me Monday."

Unbeknownst to everyone, War had his own thing brewing that evening. His and Mrs. Nobody's torrid love affair intensified. They were playing a dangerous game that they believed no one was aware of or at least that's what they thought.

During Mrs. Nobody's random stays away from home Mr. Nobody covertly monitored her every move physically as well as digitally. She was tailed to every hotel, and every dirty little meeting place of theirs. She was spied on during every carnal encounter with War.

After satisfying her sexual urges she would

return to Mr. Nobody guilt free and assuming he was unaware of her transgressions. Her voice was acidic. Her touch was noxious to him and no longer pleasurable. The green monster was beginning to rear its ugly head.

Mr. Nobody sees Mrs. Nobody walks in. "Hello darling. How was the trip? Accomplished everything you needed to?"

She smiled, nodded and lightly kissed him on the cheek. "Of course. I'm going to take a shower, dear."

He watched her slink out of view.

War left his house for a few weeks to give his brother and his fiancée some space. He took up residence at a chic hotel in the city. The visits from Mrs. Nobody increased during his stay. Bruama video called War one evening to discuss plans and caught a glimpse of a woman rolling over in bed. He made a face because the woman looked vaguely familiar to him, but he said nothing and continued talking.

In War's hotel room, Mrs. Nobody came out of the bathroom dripping wet from the shower. Steam still rose off her goose pimple prickled flesh as she stood before War allowing him to take in the sight.

She didn't bother drying off because she knew she would be wet again very soon. War sat in a chair near the balcony like a king on his throne watching as his mistress twirled around and danced to EDM music that pumped through speakers embedded in the walls.

She swayed in a trance-like state as she made her

way to him until she was within arm's reach.

He pulled her in close and kissed her stomach making tiny swirls with the tip of his tongue over the landing strip design of her pubic hairs. She shivered and moaned with each peck of his lips and brush of his tongue. As the feelings of pleasure intensified, he stood up and grabbed hold of her neck, squeezing ever so tightly and began slapping her ass.

The force increased with each swat of his hand, sending jolts of electricity through her. With each wave that surged over those nerve endings her pussy pulsated like it had its own separate heartbeat. They kissed so deeply and passionately; one would've forgotten she was someone else's property. War didn't care. She was his right in that moment. He worked his way down to her breast and bit her nipples so hard that she yelped. He then inserted two fingers into her dripping box, fingering her, flicking her engorged G spot till she came in his palm. The mixture of pain and pleasure was always too much for her to handle and she melted whenever she was around him. After hours of thrusting with pleasure and pain they both lay sweaty and fatigued. War ran his fingers through her tangled mane as he recharged his stamina for another anticipated round.

She shivered. "How do you do it?"

"Do what?"

"You know my body so well. Like you've known me forever and the funny thing is you don't even know

58

my name. It's Tavoni by the way."

War remained silent as he stirred strands of her hair around his fingers like thin spaghetti noodles.

"You know just how much I need, when and where," she said exhaling in pleasure. "I was thinking. I don't want to go home to him. He doesn't make me feel alive like you do. You should be who I come home to every night. Who I make love to until the sun comes up. I could stay here…With you….Forever…"

She looked up at him with her warm honey eyes and sighed.

"Yes, I know. It's just a dream. We live separate lives outside of here. But you can have me whenever you want me, for as long as you want me."

Just then the door to their hotel suite burst open and several men dressed in black suits rushed in. War pushed her to one side and pulled the loaded 45 tucked under his pillow. Taking aim, he quickly dropped the first two men with shots to the chest and follow up head shots. One man fell on him disrupting his shooting stance just long enough for the others to rush him.

He kicked away one of the men's guns while another shooter lined up his shot. War's lightning quick reflexes took the man by surprise. A flurry of punches distracted him from the pending gunshot coming from behind. War grappled with another shooter locking his shooting arm in place.

The gun mistakenly pointed at Mrs. Nobody,

went off sending multiple shots that narrowly missed the crown of her head by inches. She screamed and dropped to her belly as the shots ripped through the drywall. War tore the gun from the man's grip and saw the slide was locked, an indicator the gun was empty. Frustrated, he bashed the empty weapon over the guy's head until a river of red appeared. More shooters poured in. They tussled in the room destroying the T.V and lamps. Overturning the desk and chairs but ultimately he lost the fight.

A collage of hands and feet pummeled him until he was bloodied and lying on the floor squirming in pain. The remaining men bound his wrist in plastic restraints and hoisted him to his feet. Mrs. Nobody was screaming for them to let War go until one of the anonymous men drove a fist into her solar plexus violently shushing her. The wind rushed out of her lungs, and she vomited orangish bile on the fluffy white carpet. They dragged both of them down the stairs and out of a side entrance where two SUVs were waiting.

The men shoved War in one and her in the other. War was still dazed and unable to fight back as the trucks sped off in opposite directions. He had no clue how long he lobbed in and out of consciousness but when he regained his composure, he saw they were no longer in the city but taking an exit off the interstate towards a wooded area. He saw a sign that read 'Carter Air Strip, 10 miles'.

"Hey...fellas...I don't know what this is about, but you've got the wrong guy," coughing weakly.

"Shut up!"

The masked man drove his elbow into War's ribs and that action threatened to eject his dinner from his gut. There were two men sitting on either side of him and two men in the front seats. One of the men in the front radioed into what War believed was a pilot or possibly more masked assailants awaiting their arrival. Yay.

The masked man, "Inbound. 10 minutes. Start the engines. We have the package."

With minutes to spare, heading to an airfield for a destination he was unsure of, bound by the arms, and surrounded by armed men, War had little time to react.

"Hey, can someone crack a window? It's getting hot in here."

Before the man beside him could react, he leaned over and landed a vicious head butt to the guy to his left instantly fracturing the bridge of his nose. The man to the right grabbed War in a choke hold from behind and peeled him off the leaking gunman.

War unleashed a flurry of kicks that drove the broken nose guy's head through the door window, incapacitating him.

Then he rammed his body back against the man choking him. The sudden shift in weight forced the man to loosen his grip which was all he needed. War slumped in the seat and sent a devastating knee strike to the center of the assailant's forehead causing his body to instantly go limp.

War kicked at the driver causing his head to slam into the window. He reversed axe kicked the passenger who was fighting with his seatbelt. Then landed another sharp kick to the driver's noggin. The vehicle swerved left to right.

While his potential murders were distracted, nursing wounds, he pressed both of his feet against the opposite side of the SUV and shoved off with everything his legs had to yield, catapulting him and the guy behind him out the door onto the road.

They tumbled and rolled on the unforgiving asphalt, the momentum snapping the plastic bracelets binding his wrist. War scrambled to his feet and subdued the still dazed gunman, breaking his neck in one swift motion. The SUV skidded and swung 180 degrees to a stop about 40 yards away and the remaining men exited guns drawn. War pulled the pistol out of the now dead man's holster and planted clean shots in both their skulls. He knelt over the man who's neck he had broken and checked the body for spare magazines.

Finding a set of black and white photos of him in one of his cars. Another pic of him and Mrs. Nobody holding hands and walking into a hotel lobby. Another of them was taken from a window view at a restaurant. The picture that struck fear in him was one of him walking out of his beach front residence, the same beach front residence that he shared with his brother.

There was a picture of Will and Stella on the beach as well. Then it hit him. He didn't know who these people were or who sent them, but they knew of him, his brother, where he lived and who he was with.

Which meant his brother and his fiancée were in danger. War raced back to the SUV. He yanked the body from the back seat window and put the vehicle in drive. He suddenly slammed on the brakes and hopped out checking one of the bodies for a cell phone when he found one, he hopped back in the truck and took off.

He dialed his brother's number repeatedly with no response. The RPMs climbed on the dash. He picked up speed darting in and out of traffic as he sped up the on-ramp to the highway avoiding rear ending a semi-truck by mere inches as he headed to the beach front property.

Chapter 9
All Is Not Lost

The sun was coming up over the Love's Estates. Will and Stella had planned to leave the city for a few days on a getaway in the Appalachian Mountains and were up bright and early packing the car in between love taps. He'd set his phone on vibrate and left it on the kitchen countertop as he ventured in and out of the residence packing more gear in the car oblivious to his brother's emergency calls. Will was heading out the door with the last load when he stopped in his tracks.

Standing in the street were a string of men toting firearms. Stella wasn't more than a few paces behind him when he yelled for her to get down and dove back into the house tackling her to the floor right before gunshots shredded the metal and stone siding sending shards flying in all directions. Stella's scream was matched with the cacophony of bullets and mayhem.

Will shouted, "Stay down! Stay down!"

He shielded her face with his arms as glass shrapnel rained down on them. The brothers had an armory on the property but always kept guns and other weapons cleverly stashed about the house.

Will kicked the wall and a picture frame of Thor's hammer striking lightning from the heavens fell to the ground. The frame was a thick wooden border that doubled as a hidden gun compartment.

He pulled the pistol tucked away inside and double tapped the point man who entered first. A volley of rounds caused the shooters to split up and duck for cover. Will pulled Stella by her arm into the kitchen where another larger weapon was tucked away under the island. He released a latch that braced a semi- automatic shotgun to the underside of the marble countertop.

Racking the shotgun's charging handle he returned more fire, dropping another intruder who flipped over the couch from the slug's impact. A shooter had slipped in the front door during the exchange and was sneakily making his way to the kitchen through the den.

Will heard boots crunching down on bits of glass and without hesitation fired two slugs through the wall in the direction the sound originated from. Moments later a body hit the floor. The shooters reorganized and moved on the house splitting into 3 teams. Will was so focused on the men coming in through the front that he didn't see the shooters peering in through the side window.

A bullet struck him in the lower flank spinning him around. He returned a slug that found its mark in the shooter's throat as his head vanished from sight.

Stella had never seen blood in real life and instantly froze at the sight of so much surrounding her. Will pressed on the wound in his abdomen with one hand and fired and reloaded the shotgun with the other.

Another man was creeping through the back door and Stella saw him before Will. Thinking fast, she made a split-second decision and took the pistol lying on the floor and fired blindly into the man's torso. She fired multiple times and luckily one hit the intruder. Even though it took the entire magazine to do it nonetheless Will was impressed by her sudden call to actions but knew the fight was far from over and now wasn't the proper time to celebrate his fiancés quick thinking.

He moved them stealthy towards the garage shooting and moving from cover to cover dropping guns when they ran dry and replacing them with the intruders. It couldn't be that many of them left, he thought to himself, as a trail of bodies told a story.

Bodies littered the lawn and various spots on the first floor. They made it to the garage where he slammed the door shut behind them. The garage's door was reinforced steel just like the door leading to the armory.

The doors to the car were already unlocked but when he tugged on Stella she was frozen still. Shock was setting in and she was becoming frantic, bordering on catatonic. He had to slow his pace down and reassure her she would be safe and that they were ok.

Grabbing her by the sides of her head, he locked eyes with her while he spoke. He accidentally marked her beautiful face with bloody streaks that made her look like a Cherokee warrior going into battle. He tried his best to wipe away the blood, only making things worse.

They shared a moment of nervous laughter before he convinced her to get in the car.

The engine rumbled and he pulled on the column shifter throwing the car in reverse. The wheels spun hurling the car backwards through the closed garage bay door of which he didn't even bother lifting. The metal shrieked as it bent and split down the seams.

Shooters were waiting on the other side, and they opened fire on the driver's side riddling the car with lead.

The vehicle rolled to a stop in the yard. Stella was still crouched over with Will's limp body shielding her again from the fray.

She was hysterical at this point not for the men approaching but because she could hear Will's breaths were becoming sparse and heard gargling deep in his chest. She wasn't a doctor but anyone with common sense knew that wasn't a good sign and that only aided in her dread. Just as the men were closing in on them she heard tires screeching in the distance and then the crunching sound that fiberglass made smashing into a solid object.

Seconds before that, War had peeled around the corner barreling down on the band of shooters who had positioned the vehicles in their convoy in a manner that blocked the driveway. He mashed on the gas and the front end lifted slightly before ramming the broadside of one of the identical SUV's. The shooter that was using the vehicle as a cover bluff was taken by surprise as War smashed head on into him with a sickening crack that deployed all twelve featured airbags on the high-end truck.

The shooters that were lucky enough to leap out of harm's way right before the collision were scrahigh-endo their feet and moving in the direction of the crumpled transport. They couldn't get a clear view inside the cab due to the smoke and powder from the rapid airbag deployments. Four shots tore through the safety device deflating it instantly and burrowing through the neck and head of the closest shooter.

Three more rounds punched a hole through the doors side panel dropping another shooter. The driver's side door opened with a wailing creak and War appeared below the door's frame.

Two shots ripped through another shooter's legs just below the knee, causing the man to buckle and drop to one side where War lined up the kill shot, finishing him off with a bullet through the T box. War slinked out of the truck and sprinted over to where Will's car had

had come to rest.

When Stella raised her head, the men were laid out on the lawn and a figure was moving towards the driver's side. Hands gripped Will's body by the shoulders and tugged him out. A renewed sense of panic ensued her. She hopped out thinking they were going to execute him right there in front of her and she pounded on the man's back with all of her might to no avail.

When the fog in her mind cleared instead of gunmen, she saw it was War hovering over her lover. He was checking Will's wounds and vital signs.

"Help me get him in the house!"

Will was still alive but barely holding on when War laid him down on the kitchen counter. He tossed the cabinet below the sinks until he found alcohol and towels and went to work trying to stop his brother from bleeding to death.

Stella could do nothing but stand in the background shaking mortified and crying uncontrollably. Will had lost too much blood and he wouldn't make it to the hospital in time and both the brothers knew this.

Through gurgles of blood, he whispered his final words.

"Stel....la...," coughing between syllables.

War silenced him and gestured to where she stood.

"Sssh. Save your strength. She's here. She's ok bro." War knew that this was his brother's last stand.

His eyes welled up with tears that he fought back. He grasped his brother's hand in his, holding on tightly. Will signed faintly the brothers' moto. His hand wavering near his heart smearing red on the clean parts of his shirt. War pointed a finger at his head. A singular drop escaped the gateway to his soul as a tear rolled down War's cheek. Will's hand went limp.

Just like that he was gone. Stella slid down the wall plopping onto her behind and stared. It was as if time had stood still in that instance. She knelt over his body sobbing and beating on his chest demanding for him to wake up. Pleading with death to return Will to her. She stroked her blood covered hands across his still warm cheeks, unable to grasp the reality.

"William, baby, please get up. I need you. We need you." More sobbing ripped through her. "I was going to wait to tell you the good news, but you're going to be a father."

She patted her back pockets until she discovered what it was, she was searching for. A strip of black and white sonogram photos.

This news had taken War by surprise. As far as he was concerned, they were the only two remaining family members they had. Been that way for as long as he could remember and now he was hearing his brother's fiancé was pregnant. The loss of life and the beginning stages of a new life was too overwhelming right now.

War could hear sirens in the distance but none of that mattered to him right now he'd lost the best part of him and that sinking feeling was starting to settle in.

He snapped out of his trance after hearing Stella's confession and ran and grabbed a bag from the closet and came back to her.

"Stella ….We have to go NOW! It's not safe here!"

"But what about William? We can't just leave him here like this! Help is on the way. They can save him, they can save him. There's still time."

"My brother is gone!" voice cracking. "And we don't know who those men were or if more of them are on the way! Come with me, now!"

"NO! I'm not leaving him! I can't. I can't!"

He watched her treat Will's cooling corpse with the utmost respect delivering gentle touches to his hands and face. She attempted to dab away the spots of blood smearing his handsome face in between bouts of tears.

War had a moment of clarity. He could not allow himself to be detained, not with the murderer of his brother loose. Before it was all said and done, whoever was responsible would pay with their life but she wasn't part of this world and she would only slow him down. Maybe her staying until the police came was the right thing to do for her protection. Maybe that would be enough to shield her from whoever was behind this attack.

"You're right. You had nothing to do with this. The police will protect you. They'll want to take you into custody and ask you questions but that will keep you safe while I figure things out. I'm…I'm sorry."

And with that he darted out the remains of the splintered back door onto the beach.

Stella leaned over Will's body and cried not knowing what else she could do.

War watched the house from a safe distance as the police showed up in droves. He wasn't going to leave her until he knew she was safe and in their custody. He didn't want to leave his brother either, but an army of dead bodies would be impossible to explain to detectives. He observed the uniformed officers escort a shaken up Stella to a patrol car before he slipped away.

Chapter 10
Redemption Soon Forward

Miles down the road he snuck off behind a building with a metal fence surrounding the property and set down the bag he brought, sifting through the contents until he found the backup phone stashed inside. He powered it up and a message icon appeared.

It was a video message from Brauma.

There were two voices and dual images in the video recording. Immediately War recognized the other voice.

'It seems we have an issue. Someone within your organization violated my trust and my trust is not endearing nor eternal. However, my wrath is. I want you to witness something, a token of my appreciation to your employee.'

The screen flipped to show Mrs. Nobody. She was tied up to a chair. Electrical tape wound around her head covering her mouth. Blood had crusted up around one of her nostrils and blood trickled from the corner of her mouth and from a gash through her left brow. Bruises lined the tissue beneath her eyes. It was obvious she had been crying and her face was shown pure terror.

'My sweet darling. Oh, she has been naughty. Galivanting with the hired help. That's beneath you.'

Brauma's voice could be heard. 'What's this! C'mon man, I don't need to be mixed up in your sick shit relationship problems.'

'Oh, but you are. See, my lovely wife has been running around acting like a whore. In which I have been financing! She's seemed to have found someone that fancies her attention more than me.'

Mrs. Nobody struggled with her restraints and muttered incoherent words that resembled pleading.

'Sssh,' Mr. Nobody admonished before turning back to the camera with Brauma. 'She's been sleeping with your man War or Will. I can't really tell them apart; you know with them being identical twins and all. But if I had to make a bet my money it would be on War. Will seems too reserved but either way I'm going to kill them both.'

Mr. Nobody produced a pistol from his jacket and cocked the slide back. He removed the strips of tape from Mrs. Nobody's mouth, tearing away strands of hair snagged up on the adhesive side with it.

Mrs. Nobody screamed, 'You piece of shit! I never loved you! Fuck you, you little dick fucker!'

74

Mr. Nobody struck her across the jaw with the butt of the gun, bursting her lips in an eruption of red. Blood cascaded down her chin.

'Kill me! Do it already, you pussy!'

Mr. Nobody shrugged his shoulders at her outburst and grinned at the camera, then he placed the barrel on her temple and pulled the trigger at point blank range. The impact almost decapitated her, toppling her near headless body over and out of sight.

Mr. Nobody stood over her glaring down with a seething

hatred. He fired more rounds until the slide locked to the rear

then he sat the gun on the table and fixed his hair.

'Where are they?'

'I don't know. I wouldn't tell you if I did. That client confidentiality thing. Osha standards and all.'

Mr. Nobody smirked and so did the men behind him.

'Mr. Bruama, I am more than capable of tracking down those little shits and killing them myself. I thought I would make things easier for you and give you an opportunity to save yourself. Last chance.'

'Well, when you put it that way. Naw you know what I think…yea I'm sure of it. Go fuck yourself!' Brauma yelled into the camera.

Mr. Nobody began laughing hysterically.

Brauma was apprehensive at first but soon joined

75

in until the computer screen blinked out. He swatted the monitor off his desk watching the screen crack down the center distorting the image and picked up his cellphone.

"Gentlemen, I believe we were just burned. Got damnit! I don't know about you all but I really don't need these kinds of problems. I have no idea where you guys are but take my advice and lay low, this guy is well connected. I feel like a shit storm is coming. Until I can get a hold on things and what's going on..."

His attention strayed from the phone screen towards the bay window in his office.

"What in the hell is th..."

The feed cut out a split second after what War presumed was flames engulfing the screen. Bruama was gone too. War checked the time stamp and it read 15 hours ago. War called Brauma's phone, and it rang until the voicemail picked up. In that moment War was given some clarity on the situation. This whole ordeal was his fault. His arrogance and ego were the cause of so much pain and suffering.

He sat with his head down, sulking and lost on what the next move was. Planning ops was Will's thing. The realization of what transpired weighed down on him. In one swoop he'd lost his brother and the only father figure he's known all because of irresponsibly decisions he made, selfishly resulting in his world changing forever that day. Where from here? He had no idea but he had to move. He could sort all of this out when the time awarded him that but for now, he had to move. He slung the duffle over his shoulder and scaled the chain link fence he was resting up against, dropping down into a dusty tow yard.

War looked around until he found a dilapidated car suitable as a temporary hideaway and stowed away in the back seat. The rusted door slammed shut with a stiff creak. The interior reeked of rust and mildew but it was a safe location and no one would look there for him, giving him time to rest and reset his brain. Bundling the clunky duffle bag up under his head he willed his eyes shut. A whirlwind of images and memories flooded his mind. He swam in the darkness of his thoughts.

Pressure mounted on his chest, grief and regret lay with him in the back seat of that rusted van. The tears, against his will, flowed as day turned into night.

Mr. Nobody sat comfortably in a G5 private jet, courtesy of the United States Government, in a window seat overlooking a blanket of white clouds 30,000 feet above the air space, flying through the country of Oman en route to Morocco. The stewardess handed him a glass of Bourbon neat and a napkin before excusing herself. Across from him sat some of his personal security details, also indulging in drinks as the flight progressed to its destination. One of the security team's phones beeped prompting him to check the screen. There was an

incoming call. The security member informed Mr.
Nobody after the call ended that the targeted attacks on
Brauma and his assets were partially successful.

Target Alpha had been detained but managed to
terminate his captures before escaping and now evading.
His whereabouts are undetermined at this time. Target
Bravo was confirmed KIA according to police reports
coming from the local department assigned to the home
invasion case which it's being investigated as we speak.
They have one person in custody, the young lady. In
addition, target Charlie's office strike was partially
successful as well; no bodies have been recovered yet to
fully confirm KIA. The police are restricting access to
the top floors until structural integrity can be established.

"Only one half of the twins' bodies were
confirmed KIA?" Mr. Nobody asked as he sipped from
his drink relishing its crisp bite and subtle warmth.

"I have an endless financial stream of untraceable
capital which gives me the ability to purchase whatever I
need or want on a whim and yet I can't seem to find and
hire effective killers to do a simple job and erase the
existence of two men. TWO GOT DAMN MORTAL
MEN! Now, let me ask you a question. If you only have
the body of one of the men I paid good money to be
murdered and the police have custody of one of the
men's little girl friends, what does that say to you?
Hmm? That doesn't sound like a complete and efficient
wiping away of these GOT DAMN MEN'S

78

EXISTENCE DOES IT? Bring me evidence of War's dead body and kill the girl! You idiot!"

The security team member nodded and proceeded to make a series of calls.

War's eyes were shut tightly but sleep never came to him; instead, his mind was plagued with thoughts of the day and the actions that led up to his current position. It was as if someone had finally organized the file cabinet in his subconscious. Images in his mind lay out like a neat projector film that he could review. Ranging from his childhood to present day. He sat in the back of that jalopy while the reel played in his mind's eye experiencing all the emotional spectrum had to offer again. Then Stella's words played back again.

'Will, you're going to be a father.'

The word father echoed in his head bouncing off of every stress filled throbbing nerve, causing pressure to build near his temples. War was never good for anything beyond killing and therefore the idea of being a father never even crossed his mind.

Will truly was the best part of him in every way and he would've made an awesome father. He was ashamed of how selfish he'd acted originally once he found out Will's intentions to exit the business. If he would've known then that would be the last real conversation they had, it would've gone totally different. And that's something he would regret until his last days.

Suddenly he heard Will's voice in his head and it was clear as day.

'Bro, c'mon man, really? This is how you're gonna handle this? They tried to kill you. Hell, they succeeded with killing me. It was my fault. I thought I could actually get out of this shit unscathed. A fool's wish. Karma is right! Still my Stella... I knew she was pregnant. I had been tracking her menstrual cycle for weeks, you know I pay attention to everything, bro. Wow, I was going to be a dad,' laughing to himself. 'Can you believe it? Brother, it's not your fault. You are who you are and I love you for that. But now isn't the time to have a pity party for yourself. I need you, bro. Stella and my baby need you! That piece of shit reached out and touched our lives forever. What? You think he can't get in that police precinct that's holding my fiancée? Huh? Then what?'

War sat up in his seat not even realizing he'd dozed off. Was that real or a figment of his imagination? Either way the apparition was right even in the afterlife. Will was still holding down his duties as the older brother and making logical sense of the mayhem War had the tendency to create.

Stella was still alive and they probably already knew that. Which meant assets would be on the way to do one of two things and neither was in favor of her or War's future nephew or niece.

Chapter 11
Hands In The Cookie Jar

Downtown Miami-Dade
Police District

Stella sat in a small 20 by 20 foot room with the typical table and chairs in the center and the ominous oversized reflective two way mirror planted on one wall. The temperature was a chilled 63 degrees just cold enough to agitate the skin and generate extreme discomfort, a psychological tactic law enforcement personnel teach in interrogation practices.

Across from her sat a neatly dressed detective of the precinct, shuffling papers he'd removed from a manilla folder. They were photos of the crime scene at the Love's estate.

He spread each image out across the table in a neat pictogram setting so that she could see everything clearly. There were at least 30 photos of bodies, one of which was Will's. That picture of him on the counter in that manner tugged at Stella's heart strings. That emotional reaction didn't go unnoticed by the detective either, who took the opportunity to begin the array of questioning.

"Hi, I'm Detective Patrick Preston. Are you good? Do you need water? Hungry? Do you smoke?"

Stella shook her head as one gigantic response to his questions.

Detective Preston continued, "You've had quite the morning, haven't you?"

She remained quiet as the detective slid across a photo of Will, dead on the countertop in his kitchen.

"You know this man?"

She reached for the photo grazing her fingertips over Will's image as her eyes glassed over. "His name was William Love. He was my fiancé. We were supposed to get married next summer in Greece."

Det. Preston produced some napkins from his inner coat pocket and handed them off to her before he continued his line of questioning.

"And the other men? Do you know them? How about this guy?" shuffling a picture of Warren over to her. He looks familiar? Is this the same guy or a double or what? What happened at that estate? There's a lot of dead bodies, ma'am, and you're the only one alive that knows any details beyond what my forensics team can put together. So, anything that you could recall would be a big help in my investigation."

Stella knew nothing, that was obvious by her

reactions to the detective's questions. She was taken by surprise when the detective stated that numerous weapons stashes and bags of money were recovered all over the house and that the residents had an in-home armory that could rival the MDPD's.

Detective Preston eventually ran into a wall where Stella was concerned and he abruptly ended his questions once he heard a tap on the two way mirror.

The Senior officer on the other side observing the interrogation had heard enough. He knew the young lady was useless in locating Warren, but she was still a loose end and loose ends unchecked usually had the bad habit of transforming into trip hazards. He took out his phone and placed a call.

An MDPD officer sat behind an enclosed window counter with an inch thick plexiglass sheet partition separating him and the interior office from the lobby area. He was splitting his time between gobbling down chunks of a sloppily constructed sub sandwich that leaked watery mayo from the edges of the toasted bread slices, while hacking away at a keyboard when the door chime alerted him to guests entering the building. Three men approached the counter all dressed identically in black suits, white dress shirts, black ties, and hardened emotionless scowls.

The lead gentleman spoke in a grumbled tone that seemed to reverberate through the plexiglass window and quaked the pin holder sitting nearby. The stranger flipped out a name and badge that read, 'U.S. Secret Service Special Agent.'

He explained that the officers of that precinct were holding a person of interest in a string of international crimes and that they were summoned to obtain possession of the inmate and provide protection details as the inmate was being transported to a government holding facility. The officer's face wore the expression of shock even more so when the name of the inmate was given.

"Stella Renner, yea she just came in not too long ago. She was the lone survivor of a real-life shootout at the Alamo kind of incident in lower Miami a couple of hours ago. It was a bloodbath. Give me a minute and I'll find out where they placed her and open that security door for you while I'm at it."

The lead nodded and feigned a smile that oddly enough sent a cold shiver through the officer. He chalked it up to a rogue cold wind that had to have blown in when those secret service agents arrived. Minutes later the double security doors leading from the foyer into the inner workings of the precinct buzzed open. They were met on the other side by another officer who ushered the secret service agents to the elevators where they were sent down one floor to the nonviolent offenders holding cells.

This sector of the precinct housed petty violators like drunk in public, prostitutes, simple drug possession etc. They entered through another doorway that housed a row of holding cells. Dull gray painted doors with a one square foot window cut into the metal allowing the men to peer inside. Stella sat on a thin bunk bed with her knees pulled tightly to her chest. Her head buried between her arms that were folded around the top of her knees and it sounded as if she was weeping.

The uniformed officer went to key up his radio for the officer in the control room to unlock the cell holding the young lady. Just then the lights blinked out. The officer could hear the fan blades in the air ducts between the floors winding down so the power loss wasn't just in that sector, it was the whole building that went dark. Seconds after the outage, the flood/security lights burst to life burrowing dual columns of dull yellow light into the solid black surrounding them.

The exits were faintly lit up and that's where the officer headed as he radioed into the others in the building. If the power was cut the security systems had redundancies in place that would unlock all main channel way doors for access by maintenance and personnel. And would deny access to any prisoner or holding cells without a physical key until power was restored.

As the officer exited the hall and out of view the three secret service agents stood on guard with a heightened sense of awareness. Back at the front of the building the front doors opened with no alerting chimed this time and a figure briskly stepped towards the counter. The officer manning the station could barely make out the man's features in the muted light and the awful glare reflecting off the plastic window.

"Good evening, I'm here to pick up someone that was unjustly detained and taken into custody. Stella Renner."

The officer irritated, "She's a little popular tonight. Well, I'm not sure if you've noticed but we're having a bit of a power problem, sir. No visitation will be authorized, or any inmates or detainees will be released until the powers back on."

"Yea but see, she really shouldn't be in here. She didn't kill those men. I did. Well to be honest, it was the combined efforts of me and my brother, who they killed. Vengeance is on my list of things to do but first I have to make sure the girl is safe and unfortunately, she's not here. Hell, now that I think of it, whoever tried to kill me and my brother are probably already here trying to silence her. So, I don't have much time to waste dealing with you, officer."

The officer's whole demeanor changed from annoyance to disbelief. "Wait a second. How do you know about those murders? How do you know that girl?" Looking down at the papers strewn all over the desk. "What did you say your name was again?"

"I didn't."

While the men spoke, the officer was unaware

War had unfastened a 9 bang concussion grenade from his belt line and pulled the pin. He tossed the nonhazardous explosive through the tiny slot at the bottom of the window and turned his face away shielding his head from the blast seconds before the bangs went off.

The pressure wave from the concussion explosive shattered the window into tiny shards and dazed the two officers in the office.

War hopped through the ruined window opening and planted a stiff body blow to the officer closest, that curled him over like a cooked prawn shrimp lining his head up perfectly for a devastating knee strike that would've taken the officer off of his feet had War not shifted his position slightly to the side of the officers. Palming the back of his head and using the moment from the knee strike to his advantage he planted the officer's face into the linoleum countertop. The officer unconsciously slid to the floor.

The second officer was fumbling with the safety latch on his pistol when War hopped across the desk pivoting off one hand and spun around in a windmill kick that connected both of his feet to the side of the officer's head. He went crashing into a metal file cabinet with enough force to dent the side of the office, sending the officer to join his fellow in la la land.

A third officer was turning the doorknob and just breaking the threshold into the office when War spun around and front kicked the door just above the handle with all of his might. The metal door clanged shut but not before careening into the soft tissue of the officer's nose and lips instantly rupturing blood vessels, decimating bone and cartilage.

The officer was thrusted back in the adjourning wall, now bathed in mind numbing pain and fresh warm blood that poured down like an open faucet from his nose and mouth.

War quickly stepped outside just beyond the door frame and spun with a soccer ball style kick that connected to the officer's head, also punching his ticket to the dream world.

The secret service agents in the holding cell area a floor below heard the muffled pops that the 9 banger made and immediately armed up into a defensive formation. The lead agent signaled for one of the other agents to breach the exit door and investigate.

The agent cautiously crept to the door and quickly peeked out a few times making sure the coast was clear before he proceeded. The other two agents heard a muffled scream preceded by a heavy thud then silence, which made the other men tense up. The exit door cracked open slightly as two cylindrical canisters were tossed in. Disorienting gray smoke spewed from both ends of the canisters filling the enclosed space with noxious smoke.

As the agents adjusted to the rapidly changing

environment neither one of them saw War slither in behind the curtain of gray. When the lead finally noticed movement in the clouds, it was too late. War grabbed the agent in an arm bar lock rendering his shooting hand useless while he placed the barrel of his own pistol under the man's chin. A silenced pop followed a wet splat. The last agent tried to get a bead on War but he ducked back kicking the limp body of the lead agent in the way as to cause a distraction.

He melted into the smoke field as the agent let off half of his magazine. The rounds punched through the smoke cloud hitting nothing but concrete walls and floor. War fired 6 shots from another angle that stitched the agent's torso from the navel up to his forehead. Blood splashed the small window peering into Stella's holding cell. Seconds later a face appeared in the muck and smoke. Stella crouched down behind the toilet completely terrified of the chaos unraveling just beyond the cell door. Her heart felt a million times lighter when she recognized the face looking in through the window.

It was a familiar one.

"Warren? Is that you?" scrambling up from the floor. "Oh my God what is going on?! They locked me up and then those men in suits showed up and the lights went out then I just heard shots and…"

"Calm down. I'll explain later but for now I have to get you out of here. Listen, I cut the power and that makes it impossible to open the doors without a key that

I don't have. Go to the far corner and make yourself as small as possible. I'm going to have to use a charge to blow the lock. Cover your ears."

Stella didn't hesitate. She ran and ducked in the far corner, balling herself up as tiny as humanly possible. She trembled as the adrenaline spiked in her blood stream. Outside the cell, War was prepping a small disc like explosive with a magnet on one side and a turn dial with a red transparent button on the other.

He placed the device right next to the keyhole lock and turned the dial then pressed the button. He stepped back a few feet and turned away from the blast as the device counted down. The transparent node blinked red 3 times before a mild but destructive explosion occurred that sheared the head off the door's internal locking mechanism.

Inside the cell a light cloud of smoke lingered and the smell of burnt cordite. Shrapnel from the door and the locking mechanism were scattered across the floor. Stella was still in the corner crouched over. Shaken up a bit but unharmed. War slid the metal door back and stepped in, reaching for Stella who jumped at his touch. Her ears were ringing from the blast and she didn't hear him enter the confined space.

"C'mon."

"Who were those men? What's going on, War? The police, they think I have something to do with

William's murder! They…," asking a multitude of questions while getting up.

War interrupted, "They're working with the bad guys too apparently. You're only gonna be safe if you're with me. Now let's go!"

In the hall the smoke was still thick from those canisters War deployed somewhat obscuring the sight of those two agents he unlifed but it was clear from their still bodies and the pools of red surrounding them that they were dead. Stella tried her best to divert her attention away from the bodies as War guided her through the halls under that muted light.

During the pandemonium, officers rushed past them, preoccupied with the siege. Not even taking the time to recognize that War and Stella weren't fellow officers.

Tunnel vision could either be a gift or a curse. The brain becomes a one-track focused machine in times of crisis and War understood that, taking advantage of the moment to slip out. They exited out a rear door that fed into the police vehicle storage lot where War fumbled with a few car door handles till one swung open. He gently guided Stella in through the driver's side then dropped in and shut the door. Police cruisers usually keep the keys in the vehicle for easy access. Who would be dumb and brazen enough to steal a cop car on police premises, right?

War pulled down the sun visor and a set of keys

materialized in his lap like he'd made a secret wish that was instantly granted. He made sure to keep the headlights cut off while he slowly rolled through the lot undetected until he hit the street where the tires skirted before gaining traction. Stella sat quietly on the passenger side traumatized and speechless about just how fucked up her day has gotten. Then…

"Ok, talk! Tell me something! My fiancé was brutally murdered right in front of me but not before shooting and killing God knows how many people. I didn't even know he knew how to use a gun, let alone fight like some action movie hero!"
Her voice was getting high pitched by this time. "Then I get taken to the station where they're talking like I'm involved somehow. Next thing I know the lights are out and people are dying left and right. I don't even want to know how you got into a police station with a gun and explosives," flailing her hands. Her eyes got big in mid thought. "Those men in suits… They said they were secret service. SECRET SERVICE!! What the fuck is going on Warren!"

War ignored her questions and just continued driving, lost in his own thoughts as he guided the cruiser to a densely populated superstore's parking lot. Without a word he got out and walked around to her side, opening the door. She stood up and followed as the two paced from one end of the lot to the other. War homed in on the car he chose to steal. A late model dark colored sedan. He rounded the driver's side. He pulled a tool from his pocket and inserted it into the key lock.

A pop signaled to him the door was unlocked and again he ushered Stella to get in. Once she was seated, he got in, shut the door and pulled down the bottom half casing off the steering column exposing the wires and ignition switch housing. Using a straight edge knife, he drew from concealment he cut a set of wires, peeled back the plastic casing and twisted the copper pieces together. The engine sputtered to life. He put the car in drive and leisurely drove out of the lot. Again, they were silent this time for hours as the city lights turned to a rural countryside and open fields of green.

Stella almost dozed off when she felt the car drifting off the main highway. She looked up to see they were headed to a seedy rundown motel just off the highway. The type of motel that was home to meth addicts, burnt out prostitutes and serial killers. She guessed War would fit right in with the lot.

Chapter 12
Matters Of Love

The car rolled to a stop just outside of the circumference of the spotlight above the doorway leading into the motel lobby. War left the car running while he went in and purchased a room for the night. The hotel attendant was an oddly normal looking man. No one particular feature stood out about him. The strange looking gentleman was preoccupied with solving a numbers puzzle in the game book splayed across his desk when War walked in.

It took the gentlemen several seconds to recognize that his establishment had a buying customer. War looked visibly annoyed, as the clerk tinkered around with an old school cash register that refused to function properly without the gentleman slapping the side of the machine.

War paid for the room in cash because cash left no paper trails, making it untraceable. As soon as the Clerk had handed over the room key his attention returned to his puzzle and again it was as if War wasn't in the room. War left the car parked where it was and he and Stella went to a room on the first floor adjacent to the lobby where he could see the entrance and their stolen ride. War did a swift security sweep of the room. It reeked of stale cigarettes and wet carpet. The brown color scheme of the room's interior reminded Stella of a gas station if it had a bathroom lobby. The mere thought of sitting down let alone sleeping on anything made her skin crawl.

"Stay here." War said. "I'll be back. I need to get some supplies. Don't open that door for anyone. Don't even look out the window. I won't be gone long."

He didn't even wait for her to respond before he was out the door leaving her standing in the center of the room. While he was gone, she had managed to steady her nerves enough to take a much needed shower. At least they were provided with soap and it wasn't the harshest brand of soap she's ever applied to her skin. The hot shower wasn't only to wash the grim and dried blood off her skin but the soothing heat from the shower would massage her mind and give her tense muscles some semblance of ease.

She had no replacement clothes and the thought of putting back on her soiled garments made her wince but that's all she had. She was walking out of the shower with a towel wrapped around her body and another towel around her wet hair, her dirty clothes bundled up under her arm when War came back. He had a few plastic bags filled with items she couldn't readily identify.

He dropped them on the bed and retrieved a brown paper bag from one of the bags which contained a bottle of dark liquor. Stella rambled through the bags and saw there were clothes and hair dye in one bag and food stuff to make sandwiches and bottles of water in the other.

"You're a size 6 right?"

"No, I'm a 4."

"Close enough. They're already looking for me but you have to change your appearance. That's what the hair dye is for. You already took a shower and that's good. We're gonna leave first thing in the morning."

He sat down pulling his pistol from his back holster and laid it on the table. He opened the bottle and took a huge swig that barely fazed him. Stella grabbed the clothes bag, went back into the bathroom to dry off and changed clothes.

Contemplating the hair dye but reluctantly she caved. When she came back out, she was no longer a dark brunette, now it was a complementary shade of auburn. She sat down and made a simple sandwich and silently nibbled as War continued hitting the bottle. At this point he had consumed more than half of its contents.

"It's my fault."

"Huh?"

"My brother is dead, because of me. I fucked up. I fucked up. He told me my dick would get me in some trouble that my ass couldn't get me out of. He was right. Fuck!"

Stella didn't know what to do. Part of her wanted to console her fiancé's brother because the fact remains that she wasn't the only one that lost someone special to them today but also, he's been a dick since this whole thing started and he's now telling her that this whole thing could possibly be his fault. The reason her unborn child would grow up in this new terrifying world fatherless. She chose to remain still and listen for a little while longer.

"The men at the station. Those were real secret service agents. They're on Mr. Nobody's payroll. This fuck has his hands in everything. Everyone. If I would've just listened to my bro. Fuck! I can't control myself!"

He started violently slamming his fist on the table. Its wobbly particle board texture threatens to snap with each impact.

Stella was frightened at the sudden burst of rage but she knew it was from a man hurting. She rose from her seat and rested her tiny hand on his, quieting the beast, temporarily.

"Warren. You loved your brother more than anything in this world. He knew that whatever caused this, he knew you. He wouldn't blame you for any of it.

War kept his head down mostly to conceal his watering eyes as he sobbed silently. His body shuttered with every wave of tears. Then he raised his head and stared at her.

"And he used to feel the same way about me. Until you came in the picture and fucked everything up! Before you showed up it was me and my brother against the world. You made him want to be more than just us! He was quitting the family business. All for you! Just gonna leave me out here alone. I'm no good when I'm alone. You took him from me! Get your fucking hands off me!" War yelled, enraged. "I only saved your life because that's what my brother would've wanted."

Stella reels back in shock and takes a deep breath. Again, seeing the anguish behind the tears and rage.

"You're saying all of this because you're drunk and upset! I didn't make your brother do anything! He chose this, he chose us! This is what he wanted! He loved you but he needed to get away from you so he could live!" getting choked up. "Experience something other than what you two knew your whole life. He never told me what he did for a living and I felt so comfortable, so safe with him that I never felt the need to ask. He just promised me he would do his best to keep me away from it."

War took another hard swig of the bottle then slammed it back down on the table. His eye lids were even lower than before and he swayed like a man sitting in a raft in the middle of the ocean. His face had reverted back to his original emotionless state minus the stream of tears that seemed to flow autonomously from his puffy red eyes. He sniffled a few times then grabbed the bottle.

Slurring, "We were killers. The best in the business too!"

"Untouchable," he scoffed, shaking his head. "Now, if you'll excuse me, I need some time alone with my thoughts. If you need me, I'll be in the steam room."

He got up and meandered his way to the bathroom where he slammed the door behind him and turned the shower water on high burst. Stella sat there twiddling her fingertips together as she struggled to hold in tears of her own.

Chapter 13
Life Can Change In An Instant

Stella woke up the next morning half hanging off the bed. In her sleep she kicked the covers off of her and tossed the pillows to corners of the room. The fitted sheet was snatched from each corner of the bed and somehow had become untangled up on her body like a fabric anaconda. Her hair was a bird's nest on top of her head and she had to squint to keep from going blind due to the blinding strip of light slicing the space between where the hotel's cheap curtains met. Her throat was parched and she had morning breath that could wake the dead.

She peeked over, War's bed was still put together. An indicator he hadn't slept in it all night. Begrudgingly, she shoved off the bed and opened the bathroom door where she found War drunk and snoring in a half-submerged tub of cold water. The empty alcohol bottle tipped over beside the edge of the tub was a symbol that he had finished the race to get drunk before his feelings overtook him and he ended up doing something really dumb. She rolled her eyes at the sight of the drunken lunk and shut the door. There was little she could do about yesterday, and she had no idea what she was capable of doing today. Her mind was like beef stew that was missing the most important ingredient.

As the human mind works in times of crisis she reverted back to the one thing outside of William that was familiar to her and brought her joy and comfort. Coffee! She remembered last night when they got off the interstate that they passed by a convenience store right off the ramp. One of those old school truck stop establishments where you could still pump your fuel first then pay later, kind of places. She could see the edge of the store's marquee from their motel window.

There wasn't another building in sight, so this was her best and only option. She put on shoes and tiptoed out the front door intentionally keeping quiet so as not to disturb Warren who desperately needed the sleep.

It was warmer outside than she'd expected, and she could tell they were in the country by the absent scents of car exhaust and pollution, which was replaced with the sweet stinging tinge of pollen untamed flora. It was a short 50-yard walk to the store's parking lot entrance.

The store appeared even older than she originally

thought once she was inside.

The pumpkin colored floor tile had thick back grime caked in between each square. The shelves were uneven, some wider, some taller. There was a hodgepodge of items on certain shelves for sale, one shelf housed tractor trailer spike lug nut caps right next to the gum and breath mints. There were nude magazines on display in the center aisle right across from the candy shelves. It was a mess. But the one thing that store management got right was the coffee machines.

An updated assortment of ways to brew that life saving morning beverage, from a pod brewer to the slip-in trays to the original filter and coffee grounds method, the one she chose. The coffee was harsh but bold with flavor. It took a half dozen creamers and more sugar packets than she counted to bring the drink around to something akin to her masterpieces at the coffee shop but when she achieved the desired combination that first sip was like heaven.

She inhaled and immediately felt her mind drifting to her happy place. At the register an almost emaciated looking woman with stringing brown hair tied in a ponytail and a mouth missing half the bottom row of teeth grinned a gummy smile when Stella walked up. The cashier was pleasant and inviting as most country folk are. She rang her up. Stella patted her pockets trying to locate the cash she thought she had on her but quickly realized she didn't and she'd left her money in her other pants. However, she did have her card carrier containing her debit card. The toothless woman smiled and pointed at a tiny hand written sign taped to the back side of the register that read: 'Credit/Debit card usage $5.00 purchase required.' The coffee was only $1.10 so Stella quickly made decisions on snacks placed near the counter. The total amount accumulated was just over $5 and that satisfied the store's policy. Happily, the cashier rang her up.

She grabbed her bag of goodies and coffee and pranced out the door. She greedily tore into a fruit breakfast bar as she strolled back to the motel humming a tune to herself.

War's head bobbed just above the water's surface and the breaths he slowly exhaled generated small ripples that pushed out to the far side of the tub. Splashing water caused War to stir from his watery sleep. When his eyes opened, he saw a familiar face looking back at him.

Will was sitting on the toilet with a condescending look on his face. He held the empty liquor bottle in his hand while his other hand was submerged in the bath water.

"Bro, you want me to kick your ass? Stop splashing me!"

Will ignored his brother's request and splashed him some more. War protested until he fully woke up.

"Warren, really bro?" Will said with an exasperated sigh. "The whole bottle? I bet you feel like that last turd that refused to flush down the drain."

"Yea, what's new?"

"Wow bro, you picked a real shit hole to hide in. And this motel is pretty fucked up too."

"Huh? What are you talking about?"

Will looked around for a second before looking back at his brother. "Look at you. In here, alone. Drunk. While my fiancé is out there alone. I asked you to protect her. How's that going so far?"

What? She's good, bro. I bought her food and clothes last night. Changed her appearance. I know the rules. She's sleeping, bro. I'm a fuck up but not this time."

"Really? Are you sure she's safe? Laying down? Do you know what day it is? What time is it?"

War lifted his hand up out of the water and looked at his watch that had died while submerged under the water. The big hand and little hand read 4:37 but the sun was high in the sky.

He could tell from the brightness shining in through the bathroom window.

Suddenly War woke up. He was still submerged in that cold bath water. The light coming through the window indicated it was daytime but not afternoon yet, still some time in the morning. He turned to look at the toilet where the only thing that rested on the lid was his pistol. It was all a dream.

He lifted his submerged hand and looked at his watch. It stopped at 4:37. War shook his head and splashed his face with water trying to wake himself up. The room spun as he raised himself from his watery berth. Liquid cascading off his saturated clothes as he regained his consciousness.

He opened the bathroom door and to his dismay Stella's bed was empty. He reached back in the bathroom and scooped up his pistol and marched out of the room prepared to face whatever lay on the other side of that door. He glanced back and forth hoping she would be walking along the pathway in front of their room. When he didn't spot her, he paced to the front office where the clerk was preoccupied with that same paperback book filled with games and puzzles.

"Hey, buddy. Did a girl come in here today? Mid 20's. Brown skin. Auburn colored hair?"

The clerk never took his eyes away from his games and gave a one word answer. No.

War cursed under his breath and retreated back to the motel room. His clothes were wet and sticking to his body. He removed them, tossing them in the bathroom and retrieved a set of clothes out of the bags he'd bought last night. He was pulling up the zipper on his jeans when he heard a key insert into the door's lock. He froze and instincts kicked in.

Drawing the pistol, he crept to the other side where he would be concealed behind the door when it opened. The doors hinges creaked slightly as the door swung open, War pressed the barrel up against a head full of Auburn colored hair.

He didn't lower the weapon until he recognized it was her. Stella was so taken by surprise that she dropped both coffees and the bag of treats. The coffees fell to the floor splattering tan colored liquid in neat puddles that instantly absorbed into the carpet.

"Got damnit Warren! What the hell is your problem!!"

"You were gone when I woke up. The key was still here and the car hadn't moved. I thought you bailed out on me. I told you to stay your ass in this room!"

"That was last night! Jesus, Warren! I went to the store to get some coffee," shaking her head in exasperation. "With all of the shooting and death lately I needed a sense of normality in my life. I couldn't ask you to go for me because you were currently cosplaying as the last turd that didn't flush down the toilet."

That statement was familiar. War didn't respond, he just looked at her with a condescending look and sat down at the table and continued putting his shoes on... Then a thought struck him like a bullet in the brain.

"Wait. You have cash on you? How did you pay for that stuff?"

"If you're implying, I stole money from you're drunk ass the answer is no. I do have my own money. I swiped my debit card if you must know."

War froze in place. The fear of the reality of her actions spread across his face like a brush fire.

"You did what?"

"I swiped my card. What?"

War exploded, "Shit!"

He sprang to his feet and ever so gently, pushed back the edge of the curtain on the side closest to the door. From the outside looking in, that movement wouldn't have even been perceived. It was so minuscule but that small gesture awarded him the ability to see almost the entire motel parking lot and the street leading to it.

There was no movement or anything out of order, but his instincts were flaring up.

"Grab your shit!"

"What's ...what's wrong Warren?" getting scared.

War was going into overload, with every word. "The guy we're running from, I'm sure by now, has flagged all of your bank accounts! Family members phone numbers! Any social media and anything ELSE connected to you. You swiping your card was a gigantic S.O.S that's gonna tell this guy exactly where we are! We gotta go! NOW!!!"

Stella hadn't even thought about the idea that they were being tracked. Yea government agents arrived at the police precinct she was held at hours after the shootings occurred and they knew her. She had no idea how they knew her and she didn't put two and two together even after War explained somewhat to her who the people were pursuing them.

She had never been on the run before let alone being tracked by a wealthy psycho. She was still learning the rules, hopefully this infraction wouldn't cost them everything.

War was almost dragging her out of the motel room and to the car by the time she got these thoughts through her mind.

They got inside and he did his thing with the ignition wires, firing the car to life. In no time they were out of the lot and back on the main highway driving at an increasingly fast rate of speed. Stella's body braced as War drifted in and out of traffic all the while constantly glancing up in the rearview mirror.

"Warren. You have to slow down. You're scaring me. What did I do??"

"His name is Mr. Nobody and I fucked his wife. A couple times. Well, more than a couple times. A lot. A lot of times. We were having an affair and somehow, he found out."

He rummaged in his pocket and handed Stella the phone with the video Brauma sent already uploaded on the screen.

She pressed play and it became evident this was

her second time seeing carnage of this magnitude ever in her life.

When Mr. Nobody shot his wife in the head, Stella jumped and tossed the phone back in Warren's lap.

"He's a psycho," Stella said with disgust.

War nodded and glanced back up at the rearview mirror. His eyebrows furrowed when he noticed something. A spec of black over a blue cloudless sky at their 6 o'clock, about 100 feet up and a half mile trailing behind them.

"What is that? C'mon man. My luck can't be that bad. C'mon man!"

Stella started panicking again. "What? What is it?"

She turned in her seat peering through the back window at the sparse traffic behind them. She saw nothing out of the ordinary. War looked out the side mirror then back up at the rearview one more time then violently jerked the wheel to the left. Stella almost flipped over headfirst into the back seats as War swerved into oncoming traffic seconds before the asphalt erupted.

The blast blew out Stella's passenger side window and rocked the side of the car causing it to bounce on two wheels for a second before the weight of the vehicle brought it slamming back down.

War regained control and swerved again to the right, narrowly missing a painter's van that was in the lane in front of him. The van evaporated in a cloud of fire and black smoke. War mashed the gas pedal to the ground and the old sedan lurched forward as the RPMs climbed to critical levels.

Stella screamed when the second explosion went off. In the distance a predator MQ-1 drone was shadowing them lining up its targeting system for the follow up missile strike.

The drone's pilot was sitting comfortably in an air conditioned room on a military airbase in Arizona.

The pilot had been given a set of orders by his commanding officer to track a vehicle carrying two occupants who were transporting explosive material across the state. The pilot was informed that the pair were individuals connected with the Ramafa terrorists organization and were extremely dangerous if approached by law enforcement. The satisfied solution was to neutralize the threat from coordinated aerial assaults.

Chapter 14
Something Wicked This Way Comes

Poolside of an extravagant glass structured infinity pool near the ocean in the city of Santorini, Greece. Mr. Nobody sat submerged chest down in the bubbling waters of a hot tub overlooking the balcony down onto the beach below. The heated pool was filled with gorgeous women, some sporting expensive bikinis while others chose to swim in the nude. The women traded kisses and playful touches as they splashed and frolicked.

One of the sirens swam to the pool's edge, pulling herself up and over the wall as water cascaded down her smooth naked flesh. She glided over to the hot tub where Mr. Nobody was reclining and slipped in on the far side wearing a mischievous look on her beautiful face. She maintained eye contact with him until she was fully submerged beneath the water's edge.

Mr. Nobody watched from his seat as the young woman fluttered her feet like a mermaid's fins treading through the water. When she re-emerged, she was mere inches from his face. Her warm sweet breath caressed the prickly hairs of his 5 o'clock shadow with every exhale. So close in fact that their lips brushed against each other as she leveled her body up against his. He was drinking vodka and when he went to take a sip, she took hold of his hand and guided the glass over to her mouth.

She tipped his hand and the cool liquid poured down onto her plump lips. Over her chin and down her thin soft neck. The liquor pooled temporarily at the pit where her collar bones connected before overflowing and rushing down into the valley between her ample perky breasts that bobbed in the water like sea buoys. Mr. Nobody smirked and that simple expression excited her.

She smiled in turn and slowly sank below the water's surface. This time with another endeavor in mind. The sensation that woman's mouth generated made Mr. Nobody lean his head back in ecstasy.

He couldn't see but he could hear one of his men approaching from the house.

Security clears his throat, "Excuse me, sir. Our eye in the sky has located War and the girl."

The guard had a laptop in his hands with the screen already lit and facing away from him so that Mr. Nobody had a clear and unobstructed view from the pilot's POV.

He watched the drone cut through the sky as the altitude decreased, upon approach of the target. He saw the stolen sedan swerving left barely avoiding a direct hit. Fishtailing then swerved right to another near hit.

War had the sedan redlining and speeding as fast as
 it could go and he just knew any minute the old bucket would shake itself apart under the stress. He saw the aircraft line up for another shot and slammed on the brakes.

The car skidded to a stop just as the missile whizzed by overhead impacting the asphalt 25 yards in front of them. The shockwave from the blast spider cracked the front windshield and caused War and Stella to take cover under the dashboard.

The drone screamed past as it banked left to come back around for a follow up shot. Cars streaked by on either side of them blowing their horns as they fought to keep their own vehicles on the road.

War kicked the windshield out before throwing the car in reverse. The wheels spun up plumes of light-colored smoke before catching. He whipped the car around and shifted to drive again.

That play awarded them a few more minutes to come up with a plan but the window of opportunity was closing fast. The road was bare on both sides now. No buildings or tunnels or bridges to use for cover. This was it. The drone would fire a shot and that would be the end of this story.

Stella saw a pickup truck barreling down on them, heading in their direction. If War stayed on this course they would surely collide. It was a good distance away but gaining on them. It rode the center line seemingly intentionally blocking both lanes. As it got closer, they saw it was some sort of utility truck with ladders strapped to one side.

The driver of the truck must've seen the drone in the sky on a low approach because without warning they swerved and skidded to a stop sideways in the road. The driver hopped out from behind the wheel and just when Stella thought he was booking it out of harm's way he turned to rummage in the bed of the truck. Probably grabbing some important tool, he couldn't live without before bailing on the truck altogether.

To her dismay when the driver turned around he was holding a missile launcher that was hefted to one shoulder and took aim.

War at that moment was stuck between a rock and a hard place. They played him well, he thought to himself when he slammed on the brakes.

The truck driver fired and the missile blazed by streaking a thin column of smoke in its upward journey. Seconds later the UAV disintegrated in a brilliant fireball. The smoldering remains fell into a heap on the roadway. The shooter tossed the spent missile launcher back in the bed of the truck and lifted the hat they were wearing that concealed their face.

The stranger pulled out a zippo lighter and lit a half-smoked cigar resting in the corner of their mouth and it was as if a weight had been lifted off War's shoulders. The stranger walked up on the driver's side and kneeled down, exhaling a cloud that lingered in the air. A huge grin was plastered across the stranger's bruised face.

War smiled back, "Got damn old man! You almost gave me a heart attack!"

Brauma said, "Well, hello son! The party seems to find you wherever you go, doesn't it? It's good to see you're still kicking."

War got out and hugged the old man like it was his first time seeing him in years. Brauma winced from the embrace.

His body was still battered and bruised from Mr. Nobody's impromptu missile strike. Genuine relief washed over the two of them. Brauma knelt again peeking in through the mangled car window and greeted Stella with a cartoonish wave of the hand and sheepish grin.

"Hey, rough past couple of days, huh, sweety? Yea, I know the feeling." He turned back to War. "Looks like your car's burned, my friend. Need a lift? C'mon. We need to talk and now's just as good a time as any."

Poolside, Mr. Nobody threw his glass over the balcony out of frustration as he watched the drone's

116

video feed cut out after the unsuspected retaliatory strike took the drone offline.

The young woman preoccupied with giving him fellatio was shoved off after the feed cut out. A guard grabbed a handful of her satin black hair and yanked her up from the hot tub. She screamed and scampered off into the house naked, cheeks clapping together as she ran.

Mr. Nobody was incensed. "This fucking guy! Really! Really!!! That was $27 fucking million dollars!"

"Ok." He scoffed, ok…"

Chapter 15
Changes, Things Never Be The Same

The ride was cramped in Brauma's bench seat pickup truck especially for Stella who was unfortunate enough to be seated in between the two men.

She periodically glanced at Brauma, taking note of the bruises dotting his face. The bit of bandage strips across the bridge of his nose and the deep purple colors swirling around a pronounced black eye. Both his hands were wrapped in bandages. One stopped below the wrist; the other hand had four fingers wrapped together all the way up to the tips bunching the fingers together like a scooper. He had an open container of aspirins that he tossed back several times like M & M's, opting out of chasing the pills with water and rather dry swallowing the lot.

War just silently stared out the window. It seemed like his mind was in another place, a million miles away. They rode for so long that road hypnosis, the rhythmic humming of that old pickup truck's motor and the crash that occurs after an adrenaline dump in the system caused Stella to drift off to sleep.

She didn't have any idea how long she had been asleep but she woke up when she heard Warren and that old guy talking. She kept her eyes closed pretending to still be resting but her ears were perked up and wide awake.

"Brauma, you got perfect timing, always have. But how did you know where we were? Up until she swiped her card at that convenience store, we were off the grid. I trust you and all but right now trust is a rare commodity, old friend."

She felt War shift in his seat. She remained still faux sleeping.

"You want to wait till we're somewhere better to talk, cuz now might not be the ideal time for this." Brauma said.

"She's been through it all in the last 48 hours. She's in too deep now. Talk."

Brauma takes a deep breath, "Ok. Ok. After Mr. Nobody blew my shit up literally, I'd survived the blast narrowly by using my desk as cover. A hellfire rocket kicks like a got damn mule. When I pulled myself from the burning wreckage everything was destroyed. I'm sure that fuck assumed I was dead. Hell, I assumed I was dead. I got to my feet and managed to make it out of the building before emergency services arrived on the scene."

"And, that doesn't explain how you found us. You just so happened to be on that stretch of highway heading in that particular direction right as that drone strike was taking place? I'm almost tempted to ask you for the winning lotto numbers because you're lucky as fuck!"

Stella heard a metallic click. Her mind couldn't match the image of the sound to anything she'd heard before. She lay still and continued listening.

"I'm getting to that part damnit. Hold your horses. From day one I never trusted the guy. He gave me a bad vibe. Back in the agency, we had a list of gadgets and computer programs we used to monitor chat over digital transmitters. A little program called 'Project Paragon' long story short, this program grants the user access to whatever system via an easily detectable virus that's a distraction. Sort of like a Trojan horse for the program, it's complicated but basically the program is bulletproof. Ever since our first correspondence I've been monitoring his activity. Locations. Emails. Phone calls you name it. His location, numbers, and email addresses constantly change. Paranoid fuck."

"If you were monitoring his calls and emails, you know he was gonna move on me and Will?"

"No, not exactly. He never mentioned names, just call signs. I didn't put two and two together till that video call. By then it was too late. Signal went dark until a call was placed to one of his old numbers from a contact inside Miami PD."

"Oh, so you were gonna be the hero and save the girl? C'mon Brauma, that's not even your style." War said disbelievingly.

Brauma said, "You're right, it's not! I wasn't gonna save her. I was gonna follow her until she led me to him. And then I was gonna shove a rocket up his ass and pull the trigger for what he did to me! I have the element of surprise on my side. They think I'm dead! For Christ's sake look at me!"

Brauma ripped off his hat and with each passing street light the fluorescent glow illuminated his features. His head was wrapped in a bandage that was stained a light pink in places and looked like it was overdue for a rewrapping. Not only was his face bruised but there were ugly splotches of purple around the sides and back of his head as well. He was worse for wear.

Brauma continued, "I saw those secret service agents enter the building then not long afterwards you showed up. I saw you cut around the building to the rear. I didn't know it was actually you at first but once I saw the lights go out, I knew. From then on it was a waiting game. I followed you to that lot where you switched cars, smart move by the way. I knew you would do that as soon as possible. Then to that motel. If I wanted to kill you, trust me I would've. I had plenty of opportunities."

"How did you know the girl would fuck up? We were clean, underground. I know how this goes."

"She doesn't. She's a civilian. She doesn't play by our rules. I knew eventually she would fuck up for that reason and she did. Which was good on our part. That credit card signal was picked up by his scanners and rerouted to his network. Which means I know his current location. I have my program tracking the signal off a cellphone in the Mediterranean. I know where he is!" Brahma finished breathing heavily.

War was silent for a long while. Stella assumed he was thinking about what the old man had said to him. After a while he simply replied with an "Ok."

"So, you gonna put that thing away or point it at me for the rest of the night because trust me. You'd only be
doing me a favor, bud."

Stella cracked open one eye and saw that War had his pistol pointed at the side of Brauma's head. The sight of the gun startled her and both men noticed. War de-cocked the hammer on the long semiautomatic pistol and slid it back in its holster.

"Great! Now that that's settled, I could sure go for some breakfast. You hungry? I'm hungry. How about you all?"

They arrived at a diner that looked like it was a

couple decades behind the times. There were cars in the parking lot and the lights were on, so Brauma pulled in. It was warm and inviting on the inside surprisingly enough.

There were two waitresses on hand working both sides of the nearly empty establishment, while the cook in the back banged pots and pans as he prepared meals. A sign at the front of the store said, 'seat yourself'. They chose a booth seat in the rear corner that gave them a view of most of the diner including the front entrance and the swinging door leading into the kitchen.

A set of small 19 inch box shape televisions were suspended above the floor in two corners of the diner. They were tuned into the local news station where the news anchors were describing the hectic scene of a terrible gridlock on I-27 due to a tractor trailer fire some hours ago that shut the whole highway down. The traffic chopper's view showed that traffic was backed up for miles and countless county police blocked off the road.

Stella nervously looked at War and then to Brauma. Both men smiled and shrugged their shoulders. Apparently, this wasn't anything new to them. Cover ups and conspiracies were a part of their lexicon.

Stella exclaimed, "That wasn't a damn truck fire though!"

A plane was shooting at us. For God sakes you blew it out of the sky with a rocket launcher thing! Who rides around with a rocket launcher?!? You! You actually ride around with rocket launchers in the back of your piece of shit truck like it's a tool kit?!?"

Brauma shrugged as he took the first sips of coffee from the fresh mugs the portly and remarkably jolly waitress had just poured up for them. "Happens pretty often to be honest with you. Mostly they put the blame on Semi tractor accidents."

"Or plane crashes," War said.

Brauma jumps back in, "Or Train derailments."

War added, "Or random shipwrecks."

"Or being taken captive by roving pirate ships," Brauma chuckled.

"Or Nuclear power plant meltdowns."

Brauma ends with, "Black outs or energy grid issues. It's all mostly cover ups for something way bigger. Trust me. We both have been the cause of quite a few of those in our lifetime." Laughter ensued.

Stella again found herself stunned into silence as the men laughed and then ordered meals. How could they possibly have appetites after the things they have experienced today? They took the liberty of ordering her something as well.

The meals were consumed in relative silence. Once the last bite was taken, the bill was paid and the trio piled back into the truck to continue the last leg of their journey.

A while later Brauma turned off the highway into an eerie looking back road that turned from smooth black top to ruddy uneven dirt roads that descended down the hillside in a gentle grade, bottoming out at the base of the valley.

Ahead of them maybe a half mile sat a lonely single wide trailer propped up on cinder blocks. It was positioned 20 yards from a small river that gurgled surprisingly loud for its size.

There were a couple of weather worn lawn chairs and a tiny square shaped barbecue grill in front of the spring loaded screen door. Stella slid out of the seat and looked around.

Besides them and the trailer there wasn't another soul or structure in sight. Nothing but trees and God's country. Above the trailer home sat a comically large satellite dish pointed away from the setting sun. She heard a low steady rumbling noise like that of a small motor running behind the trailer.

Brauma spoke, "We're here! Home sweet home. What do you think? Beautiful right? C'mon, let me show you around!"

Beautiful? The puzzled look on Stella's face must've said out loud what she was quietly thinking because
Brauma stopped mid stride and addressed it.

"What? Yea she needs a little love. Some cosmetic treatment and maybe new siding but what she lacks in beauty she makes up for in comfort and mobility. This is my mobile command center."

They weaved past the lawn decorations and up the short double set of wooden steps. Inside, the trailer looked like any other typical trailer. Bedroom and a bathroom room to the right. A small living room and kitchen combination front and center and another room to the left. From the general location of the living room, you could easily see the entire tiny space.

A series of lights flickered from the room to the left, catching Stella's attention as Brauma opened the fridge and removed a few cold beers. That's when he noticed the direction she was staring in. He casually shut the door as he handed off the cold beverages. Stella just held hers awkwardly as the men talked and guzzled theirs.

War looked at Stella, "Hey Stella there's a shower back there. Brauma said there's towels and a washcloth as well. I gotta talk to the old man and find out what else he knows. Go get cleaned up if you want."

War and Brauma slipped away into the closed off room making sure to shut the door behind them. Brauma sat down at a computer desk and punched a few command prompts on the keyboard and the screens lit up.

There were 4 main monitors, each displaying a different set of information: global maps with live tracking, to digital phone records of incoming and outgoing calls, weather patterns and one screen was the point of view from a camera disguised as some sort of head wear. The focal point kept going in and out but the image was a mountain side with what looks like a castle carved into the ancient rock.

Brauma started pointing at the screens, "I've been live tracking our man since day one like I said before. The red pings are locations that he's visited. The blue ones are locations that he revisits. The black ping is the location he frequents the most. This monitor is a mini cam fashioned into a worker's helmet aboard a merchant ship that passes through the waterway daily according to the GPS longitudes and latitudes. The fucking guy has a literal fortress.

No bullshit compound in the jungle. Not an actual Middle Age rock and stone fortress. Fucking prick."

War studied the images of the fortress as Brauma pulled up a blueprint and schematics of the structure.

"What do we got for defensive and offensive measures?"

"Everything!"

He explains that the fortress is living up to its name and intended purpose. "The bowels of the fortress spill out into the Red Sea. Surface level there's armed patrol vessels on constant rotation and they have green lights on anyone or anything that infringes on those waters. Below the surface is where the real dangers lie. 20 yards below there's a floating mine field. Installed into the rock face is a series of torpedo tubes loaded with

MK48 Mod7 CBass making water insertion impossible. On the roof there's five SAM stations strategically placed to cover every angle of the structure from the air. Along with those beauties there's three 25mm automated turret cannons. The courtyard surrounding the fortress is also a minefield. Inside, there's four levels not including the basement where Mr. Dipshit has converted the whole space into a panic room equipped with an escape hatch that exits out into the storm water drainage tunnels but those are gated off from the outside and are at the water's surface level again. Impossible to cut away without being noticed. There's an elevator that runs the length of the structure top to bottom so in case of an emergency he can take the redline south in a hurry. The building has its own energy supply so there are no external forms of manipulating the power. A literal fortress."

War studies the pictures flipping from frame to frame as his mind became a Rubik's cube. Spinning and forming endless equations until all sides are solid enough to be called a plan.

"What's the max ceiling height on those SAM station's radars?"

"25,000 feet. Why?"

"Those SAM's can't detect body size targets correct?"

"That is correct, you crazy son of a bitch. In order to do what I think you're planning to do you'll have to drop from an altitude no less than 30,000 feet for the safety of the plane and pilot. That means you'll need cold weather jump gear, an oxygen source with a rebreather along with everything else you'll be hauling for this op. The SAM's won't be able to detect you but those 25 mm turrets can and will and if they do, well, you're confetti."

War calculated, "If I punch through the radar floor fast enough the turrets won't have a chance to scan and pick up my signal."

"Yea but you're talking about deploying a chute at under 1000 feet after moving at 120 miles an hour. You're a madman but that's just suicide."

"I know. It's so crazy that no one would attempt it. Perfect. And there's standard HVAC units on the roof, correct? No reason to do it up in that department if you don't think anyone would ever make it that far right?"

Brauma nodded because he could see the twisted plan unfolding in War's deranged mind. And it excited him. He felt like he was back in the field. Little did he know that was
exactly what would be required of him.

"Listen. Me and my brother would have executed this with no problem. But he's not here. And that leaves you, old man. I'm gonna need you on this one." War said seriously.

Brauma looked up at War and just knew the look on his face meant business.

"Normally I'd say fuck no. But this one's for Will. What do you need?"

War took a small beer break before getting into the meat of the planning phase. He was retrieving an ice cold one when he heard sniffling coming from the other side of the trailer home.

He peaked in one of the other rooms where Stella was trying to quietly sob into her towel. She stopped when she saw War's head pop in. He said nothing, he just sat down beside her and they stared at the floor. He reached into his pocket and pulled out a set of car keys and a piece of paper that he looked at once before handing it to her.

"What's this?" Stella asked.

"Keys to a new life. No pun intended."

He nodded to the front door and she instinctively knew what he was talking about. She laughed a little bit before reading the piece of paper. It was a series of numbers in two rows.

"The beater is mine now?" laughing again. "Great, always what I wanted. Missile launcher included. What's this paper with these numbers on it?"

"That is the access code and account numbers for a
storage box in the vault of Global Republic Bank of Cayman.
In the Cayman Islands. The storage drawer has a key in it that opens a vault in the bank. Inside the vault is a little

over 3 million dollars U.S currency and a few hundred thousand in bearer bonds. Enough to kick start a new life."

The look on her face became solemn as she understood what he was conveying to her.

"You're...you're not coming back from this one, are you? This is your way of saying goodbye."

He didn't respond. He just took another healthy gulp of beer and stared at the floor again. Through all the things she has been through with him and his brother, she was finally understanding.

She had to admit to herself that her original impressions of him were wrong. She thought War was an egotistical jackass. A pretty boy with a tough guy complex. Anything but the caring and enduring guy that's sitting next to her.

Right now, he almost seems human.

Stella said, "Warren, you're a good man. You deserve a good life. You don't have to do this. You can run. I'm nobody. They won't look for me and you seem like you can handle yourself pretty well."

"I'm not a good man... I'm trying to do something good for once in my life. Maybe I can work on that afterlife retirement plan my brother used to talk about once this is over. Hey, listen. Once you get that money, you vanish. Change your name. Start over..." He paused. "Thank you for what you gave my brother. He deserved it. He deserved you."

With that he got up and walked out but not but
not before
patting her on her shoulder. His way of reassuring her
things would work out.

Chapter 16
The Mouse And The Trap

A plan was hatched that evening. They would acquire the aircraft from a privately owned airbase that Brauma just so happened to know about and insert themselves over Mr. Nobody's airspace.

They had to move quickly due to the nature of the target and his inability to remain in any one place for extended periods of time. Bruama swore that he believed Mr. Nobody suffered from a severe case of ADHD.

The plane they 'acquired' was a long haul cargo freight liner. The kind that parcel delivery couriers used to transport overseas goods and wouldn't raise suspicions to see a cargo freighter overhead.

Inside the cargo bay the lights would shift from green to red when the bay was unpressurized and in high altitudes, alerting the pilot and potential crew that the cargo area wasn't safe, or permission granted to enter the space without a breathing apparatus.

In this case the shift light signaled when the team would be over the designated drop zone. A free fall dive at zero one hundred hours in pitch black darkness from an elevation of 30,000 feet plays tricks on the human mind. The rushing wind and the appearance of stopped motions makes you feel like you're suspended in air. Stay focused. Keep your eyes on your altimeter. Cold temperature Frog suits, dive helmets and goggles will shield you from the frigid elements.

The suits come equipped with glider wings to negate the high-altitude fast speed drops and brake in acceleration, giving them a measure of control as they mitigate the momentum coming in. They would get as close as possible to the fortress before deploying emergency chutes.

The sudden snap back of deceleration is brutal on the mind and even worse on the body but necessary, otherwise they'll sling shot right over the target LZ and increase the probability of being detected.

Once boots are on the deck, they have 30 seconds to remove the maintenance hatch to the HVAC unit and wiggle down into the air ducts gear, all before the surveillance cameras sweep and pick up their presence.

Once safely secured in the air duct, the pair will split up. War is the younger agile one, so he will head to the elevator shaft where he will access the tunnel, attach drop lines and repel to the level just below the basement where the structure beams that support the whole fortresses weight are exposed.

There he would strategically place plastic explosives on each of the 16 beams associated with distributing and stabilizing the weight of the structure. Once complete, he will ascend back up two stories to the first floor where he will hide and wait for the signal. In the meanwhile, Brauma would be working his way down from the 4th floor which happens to be Mr. Nobody's private quarters.

This entry point was chosen because even a savvy international spy dealing in weapons, drugs, murder, governmental classified intel and anything else you could imagine, requires his privacy.

Every floor of the fortress is heavily surveillance except the top floor. The third floor houses the security control hub center. Brauma would carefully skate around the cameras only choosing to engage with hostile if deemed absolutely necessary. When he reaches the hub, he'll enter and eliminate the guards posted on duty probably preoccupied with watching the monitors and not particularly zoned in on the killer walking in behind them.

Silenced tactics are preferred.

Once the threat is eliminated, he'll activate the rooftop security measures along with tripping the courtyard minefields. Brauma will designate Mr.

Nobody's transport vehicles and outside patrol as enemy combatants.

Mr. Nobody would be in the spacious kitchen area taste testing a veal dish prepared by his personal chef unaware of the ambush in place. The young calf meat is tender and flavorful as he closed his eyes to revel in the amazing flavor when a cacophony of gunshots and explosions commanded his attention.

Through the large bay kitchen window, he would observe his transport vehicles under attack as bullets riddled the roof and hood. The vehicles go up in flames like lit matches. The guards on foot scrambled for cover but to no avail as the large 7.62 rounds made short work of them. The sewing machine style rhythmic cadence of the guns transforms those men into quivering piles of warm red flesh as the minefields explosions provides the perfect distraction and lends a compelling argument for a need to retreat to the panic room according to safety protocols, which dictate that in the event of an invasion from overwhelming forces, he is to be expedited there and would be locked down until the threat subsides.

War would be lying in wait and once the opportunity presents itself, he would spring into action. Bullets would stitch the guards surrounding Mr. Nobody, taking him totally by surprise. This would boost sulfolipids, a fear producing chemical in humans, which disrupts the logical thinking portion of the brain. Mr. Nobody's reinforcement would arrive as planned.

Mr. Nobody will take the coveted time to reach the entrance to his safe room once using his hand scanner where it will gain him access to the room. Once the door closes, that's it. He will be beyond his assaulters reach. At that point War will remove his face covering revealing his identity.

Mr. Nobody will immediately recognize the threat and begin to formulate a retaliatory response. At that point War will inform Mr. Nobody of the pending doom and his current predicament. The mouse and the trap.

But as any good tactician knows the best laid plans of mice and men often go awry.

War's plan never left the ground, metaphorically speaking. He had been taken for the fool long before the fortress assault would be a thought. While in the solitary space of that cargo plane's storage bay, both men quietly reviewed the plan in their minds. For War, he also revisited what led to the start of all this and what it cost him thus far when a singular thought materialized. How?

Strange how such a simplistic question can yield even more complex responses. How did things progress this far out of whack? How did he end up entangled with the wife of such a powerful man? How did he disregard the red flags? But then those thoughts took a turn down a road in his consciousness that hadn't been previously explored. How did those shooters know SHE, Mrs. Nobody, was with him? She did keep a phone with her but from what he remembered every time it rang, she discarded it.

Yes, cell phone signals can be triangulated but that night at the hotel she didn't have her phone with her at all. She didn't bring anything with her up to the room because he was the one that rented the hotel suite for the evening and didn't give her the address until he was already in the room. He had his phone though.

And how did they know where Love's Estate was? Will and War were very meticulous in keeping that a secret that only a few held, not even Brauma knew where they rested their heads. Brauma's words echoed in War's mind, 'Back at the agency we had a list of gadgets and programs we used to monitor digital transmissions' 'Project Paragon' 'It was a Trojan horse for the program' 'You would never know your equipment was infected with it.'

Would Brauma have used such a program against the twins? But how would he have known about the police station before whoever called into Mr. Nobody? War saw those secret service agents enter the Miami precinct before him. That's why he waited to strike. The video of Mr. Nobody executing his wife was sent to every phone the brothers possessed, including the ones stored in their go bags. But it was encrypted, all their devices were. Until he opened that video of Mr. Nobody killing his wife. War still had that same device on him at that very moment and it's been with him since the police station. Son of a bitch! The reality of it all socked him in the mouth.

Just then War's eyes opened to find sitting across from him was his old friend. Their eyes met. Apparently, he was being watched for who knows how long.

Brauma spoke, "Hey, sleepy head. I was just about to wake you up. We're 10 minutes out from the drop." He continued to look at War. "Hey, you alright? You look weird."

The two men were dressed out in full tactical gear beneath their frog suits. The only thing exposed was their sidearms set in thigh holsters and rifles strapped across their chests that hung in a nonthreatening manner.

The rest of their equipment, chest protection rigs stuffed with rifle and pistol magazines, small explosives ordinance, med kits, and any other items that might have been needed for the mission were concealed beneath the jumpsuit.

War noticed that the safety strap that held Brauma's pistol in place was unfastened. That's a rookie mistake, not something a seasoned field operative would do. Habits like this are hammered into you during training. You only intentionally remove the safety strap when you're about to engage with it.

"Hey old man, your pistol is unlatched."

Brauma looked down and genuinely seemed

surprised as he reset the safety strap, testing the retention by tugging on the handle a few times.

"Ha, rookie mistake. I guess I'm rustier than I thought."

War pulled out his cellphone and activated the screen. He scrolled to the pics that Mr. Nobody sent of his beloved brother Will. He lingered on the photo for a quiet minute recalling the good times and memories they shared. Seeing his brother on the screen alive reignited the pain in his heart at the loss of his twin. He stared at the screen long after the backlights dimmed and it was just his own reflection staring back at him.

"Why?"

Brauma was preoccupied reviewing some intel on his own device when he heard Wars solitary question.

"Huh? Why what?"

"Why?? My brother didn't have to die."

"No, he didn't. But you'll make amends for that lost brother. A life for a life. You better believe it."

"You're not getting it. I'm asking you why. It didn't hit me until just now. I guess it was so much going on that my mind didn't catch up. Catching me with Mr. Nobody's wife. The ambush at our place. The police station. The highway chase. How did any of that come about? I'm…we're…. me and Will were always so cautious. This phone has been with me since his death. Had it with me the whole time. It's the one thing that ties into everything else. That and you."

"And me? And just how do you figure that one son?"

War kept his head down, staring at his reflection as he spoke. Feeling the furnace in his stomach beginning to heat up.

"I didn't see it at first, with all the other distractions occurring around me and I probably never would have if you hadn't said something. But I was thinking about the hotel and what happened that night. Those gunmen knew exactly where we were. They knew my name. They called me by name when they pulled me into their truck. Even the drone strikes on us was weird and then you magically show up with a Javelin rocket system. Right equipment. Right place, right time huh? Naw, that's too easy. So again, I'll ask you one more time. Why?"

Brauma's face showed a level of confusion as he pondered on the list of questions presented to him. Someone untrained in the art of reading body language might have fallen for the act but War could see the signs, the tells like in a poker match that Brauma unconsciously tried to suppress.

The subtle twitching in the corners of his mouth. Eye contact but not quite dead in the center, more like he was staring at a singular point. Perhaps the space between War's eyes to give off the notion that he was holding eye contact.

The emotionless facial expression. No human is always in complete control of their emotions, especially when being accused as the reason someone lost a loved one, that would push anybody to react. But Brauma's face remained still, frozen.

Then just like that the ploy melted away as an ominous grin developed on his face. His brow furrowed and his eyes became more sinister.

Chapter 17
All Is Fair In Love And War

"Bravo son, Bravo. I honestly didn't think you had the capacity to see it all. And to think I was really sitting here thinking you would take this whole trip with me before you put it all together, if ever, and found out the truth. The truth is that this isn't a mission to kill Mr. Nobody but actually a move to capture and deliver you to him. I'll give it to you; your brother has always been the smartest one. I gave you the benefit of doubt for that reason alone. And here you are proving me wrong. Good job, son. Damn good job."

War went to unholster his pistol but Brauma was quicker planting a front kick to Wars' dominant side that shifted his whole body then a swift roundhouse to the jaw sent him tumbling off the seat onto the graded steel deck with a painstaking thud.

War tried a sweep attack that Brauma knew was coming and dodged the attack before planting a stiff knee strike. War blocked the move however he wasn't ready for the follow up front kick to the lower jaw that sent him sprawling back across the deck.

War spat a wad of thick saliva mixed blood onto the deck and wiped away the excess with his hand. He sprang up on one knee ready to present his pistol when Brauma side stepped him, arresting War's arm in an arm lock and in one motion flipped him over onto the bench. A hollow pang reverberated down the entire length of the bench and in War's head. He was dazed as his world faded in and out.

"Now this is a surprise. I'd have bet my money you would have been kicking my old ass up and down this walkway and not the other way around. I'm disappointed, really I am. Guess wisdom really does beat youth out. But anyway, to answer your question. It's because of you, son. You and your uncontrollable urge to fuck, everything! You're like a pitbull with the pink thing hanging out."

He let loose an elbow strike that War was cognitive enough to block and he traded off with a knee strike of his own that smashed into Brauma's jaw. The maneuver created some distance between them. Brauma had to shake off its effects as he worked the hinges in his jaw left to right. The pearly whites of his teeth now tinted a bright red.

Brauma grinned, "Nice. See, here's the thing

about our friend Mr. Nobody. He is somebody. With a shit ton of money to burn."

War threw a three punch combo that Brauma dodged, slipped, then parried into a punch combination of his own.

Brauma continued as he and War maneuvered. "The guys a dick but he's loaded. He could've set us for life. But after your antics, not only did he not want to work with us any longer, he blackballed us out of the business. I only had two choices if I wanted back in, really one. When I was forced out of the agency, I didn't have a clue what I would do. All these skills just sitting on the shelf? Naw. I'm really good at death and espionage. I'm older now so I can't move like I used to but I'm doing pretty good for an old man, right?"

War faked a roundhouse kick only to deliver a devastating spin kick that crumpled Brauma to his hands and knees, gasping for breath. War went in for another kick strike but Brauma blocked it and rolled off to the side taking War's leg with him. War slammed into the hull of the plane and before his mind could register the pain, Brauma delivered kidney shots that chopped him down like an oak tree to a logger.

"For what it's worth your brother wasn't the one that was supposed to die, that truly was an accident. It should've just been you and the bitch. But you know how the saying goes. Can't make an omelet without breaking a few eggs. So, another plan was hatched. If I deliver you to him all nice and neat and wrapped up with a pretty red bow, then we could get back to business. Me and him of course, because you'll be dead. Unfortunate really. It's so difficult to find good workers in this economy."

Brauma went for the final blow but War stepped into the attack. He buried a rib shattering blow to Brauma's mid-section then stepped in further hooking an arm under and around Brauma's inner thigh.

He propelled himself upward with his legs launching Brauma in the air. His head connected with the ceiling splitting the scalp down to the bone right before War caught him and tossed him into the wall. Situated on that very same wall was the release button that lowers the plane's bay doors.

Alarms blared to life as the door began opening, zero temperature winds whipping and gusting up into the pressurized space. Beyond the bay door was a sea of black.

The roar of the engines rivaled the swirling air. Brauma swiped his hand over the crown of his head and wasn't shocked when it came back covered in blood. He smiled as he struggled to his feet.

"Nice move. You aren't such a pushover after all, huh? Look, I'll make you a deal. Surrender now and come peacefully and the girl can live. We don't even want her anyway, she was just bait to lure you in. Whaddaya say?"

War didn't respond.

Brauma's smile morphed into a scowl as he drew a pistol from concealment and fired shots. War missed the first two shots by a hair's length and caught the third round in his right flank. The two stray rounds punched holes in the hull separating the bulkhead from the cargo bay. Immediately the plane nosedived.

One or both rounds had struck the pilot in the back, killing him instantly; his body lay slumped over the controls which were now pushed as far forward as they could go. The systems alerted of pending danger and an immediate request to pull up message repeated over the speakers. The increase in G force due to the sudden nosedive flopped the men around the cargo bay like pancakes.

Brauma was stunned but quickly regained his composure and crawled to where his chute pack was stored near the bench. Strapping the pack on he crawled further to the bay door. He glanced back to see War laid out on his back, the front lower half of his shirt was soaked in blood and the stain was growing. He looked around for Wars chute and when he didn't see it, he chalked it up as it probably slipped out the bay door during the scuffle. With one last glance over his shoulder, he pulled himself up and over the ledge and out into the dark.

Plummeting from 30,000 feet, ice cold and bleeding from the head. Mr. Nobody's not going to appreciate the fact that War died by someone else's hand but that's a problem for another day, thought Brauma as he righted himself and rapidly descended.

A heavy force crashed into Brauma from behind causing him to spin like a windmill. When he stabilized, he saw it was War barreling down on him for a second strike. The crazy son of a bitch leapt from the plane without a parachute. Brauma tried to dodge the blow, but War reached out and grabbed the chute straps. The men tussled, spinning around in an endless circle as they fell closer to earth.

War, still holding on to Brauma's chute straps, pulled his knees in close and propelled his legs upward in a piston motion that knocked Brauma unconscious. His limbs flail wildly in the rushing wind. War narrowed his physical profile making him more aerodynamic and cut the distance of the two in half in seconds and was right back on top of Brauma, who was coming back to consciousness when he felt legs wrap around his waist and then his waist strap disengages.

He felt an arm slide in between his and the parachute pack. When Brauma opened his eyes, he saw War working his arm into the space between the strap. Brauma grabbed at him and tried to wrestle him off but War was stronger now.

"Hey kid. Listen. I'm sorry…I'm sorry about your brother's death and trying to kill you. The lies. All of it.

Please. Don't do this."

"Well you know the saying. All is fair with Love and War."

War yanked the knife seated on his chest rig and plunged the blade into Brauma's chest. Then without warning cut one of the straps binding the old man to the parachute. The G force pushed Brauma right out of the comfort of the parachute harness and into the wide open skies. His scream echoed until he was only a pin prick in an ocean of black.

War was wounded and bleeding steadily but he managed to wrap one arm around the backpack harness and he used the same hand to pull the cut strap across his chest. He yanked on the rip cord and a tight jerk signaled the chute was filling with air. As he floated into unfamiliar territory below he saw the cargo plane drifting towards the horizon and out of view.

Chapter 18
Cashing Out, Guardian Angel

Six months later

Stella stood in front of the large revolving doors that led to the Republic Bank of the Cayman Islands as she drilled her nerves before entering. The central bank's main floor was large and spacious with a dozen tellers assisting customers at each counter.

A man in an expensive suit approached Stella inquiring if he could help her. She could barely understand him through his thick Caribbean accent at first but she informed the gentleman she was there to do a withdraw from a vault that she inherited from a deceased loved one.

The gentleman directed her to a collection of customer service offices at the back of the sales floor. There a woman took her down name and account information. Once the account was verified, she motioned for Stella to come with her. She was led to a gated off room which required a digital key code password that Stella provided from the sheet of paper War had given her.

Once inside the clerk browsed through a collection of number plated drawers until she found the one corresponding with the account number Stella had provided. She pulled out a slim metal box and sat it on the table. She instructed Stella that the vault room was the next room over before she excused herself shutting the chamber doors on her way out.

The box's interior was lined with soft burgundy felt and a silver key sat in the center of it. Stella removed the key and found the vault in the next room. There were four vaults in total. The vault door was slightly bigger than a file cabinet.

With shaky hands she unlocked the door and pulled the first drawer out revealing three identical black shiny boxes with engraved handles on top. She flipped back the lid on the first box and almost fainted at the sight. Crisp hundred dollar bills tie together in bundles of $10,000 demonization neatly stacked in rows of five across and five rows deep for a sum of $250,000.

Four drawers set up the exact same way equaling 3 million in cash. There was also a briefcase with stacks of government bearer bonds like War had mentioned. Tears of joy welled up as memories of Will filled her mind then his brother Warren, and whatever sacrifices he made to spare her life.

Stella had reconstructed the bank accounts so only she had access to the full sum. Overnight she became a millionaire.

She took War's advice and not only left the state but the entire country. The world was a big place and she decided it was her time to see it in all of its glory. She changed her name and eventually she settled in Ontario, Canada.

She purchased a building that she renovated and turned it into a coffee shop of her very own. She had Will's baby; it was a boy. She named him William Warren Love for the two men. The brothers that changed her life forever. She named her cafe, Starry Skies, as an ode to the night she rode with William on the back of his motorcycle. The night that changed everything.

In little to no time the cafe was doing extremely well. She had a handful of employees that all enjoyed working under her. Her baby was healthy. Life was good.

On those late nights she wished Will's arms were holding her tight and sometimes if she wished hard enough, she could actually feel him. Smell him. It was odd but on cold nights she embraced it.

She also wondered where Warren was. Did they give him a proper burial? Was he finally at peace? These thoughts frequently circulated through her mind but she never let them be known. Her thoughts were hers to treasure and safeguard from this world. This world that took the love of her life but also replaced that with a new love. This world was far from safe, but also beautiful in its own ways.

———————

One day while at the cafe, a gentleman entered. He was very clean cut, well put together and spoke softly. His hair was slick back and it made him look important. Stella couldn't explain the why but that's just what she felt.

He wore a suit with no tie and carried a bricfcase. He was pleasant when he ordered as Stella was his barista. He took his order and sat at a table near the window. For hours he typed away at his computer refilling his coffee mug a few times as well as ordering food items. Stella assumed he was writing a book or a term paper or a business proposal; he just looked like the type.

He must've been really into his work because time flew by. He hadn't realized the cafe was rounding up to closing time until Stella approached his table.

He smiled and apologized for overstaying his welcome and Stella laughed it off. She understood what happiness is when you're comfortable and she asked him to please come back again and see her soon. He promised he would very soon and smiled again on his way out. She locked the door behind him and turned back to finish her managerial duties.

Unbeknownst to her there were a few cars left scattered in the parking lot, one belonging to her and the owners of the others were a mystery. The well-dressed gentleman had approached one of the cars, where a shady looking man with a low haircut and a clean shaven face decorated with scars was chain smoking cigarettes to the point a pyramid of burnt cigarette butts were accumulating outside of the driver's side door.

"Yea, it's her. There's a half dozen employees inside. Boss said he didn't want it to be messy, so we'll follow her home and do it there."

Her last employee left but not before offering to walk her to her car. She politely declined telling him she was ok. The employee insisted but she continued to decline and finally the employee yielded and left. When it was her time to go she set the alarm, locked the doors and headed to her car.

It was late and a chill breeze swiveled through the nearly empty lot. The sun had set and as she walked the length of the parking lot, she noticed a car parked a few spots down from hers.

The driver's side window was rolled all the way down, which was strange for this time of night in an empty lot. There was a pile of cigarette butts right outside the window but the car was vacant. She looked around briefly before continuing the walk to her car. She glanced around one last time before she hopped in and drove off.

154

The car parked behind hers in the next row looked empty from the outside, but it wasn't. A pair of familiar eyes stared back at her through the rearview mirror undetected in the low visibility and heavy reflections from the streetlamps.

War smiled as he saw his brother's wife notice the strange car in the condition it was in, the pile of cigarette butts and even checked her surroundings before she got in her car.

"Good girl. Staying vigilant. My brother taught you well."

Muffled murmuring came from the back seat of his car and his attention was diverted to that same clean cut well-dressed suit guy from earlier, except he wasn't so clean now.

His left eye had a deep red ring around it. The bridge of his nose was obviously broken by the crooked bulge protruding beneath the skin. Blood from his nostrils bled down over the silver duct tape covering his mouth. More blood seeped through the spaces between flesh and tape around his mouth.

His hand and feet were bound together and the collar of his crisp white under shirt was stained red all the way up to under his chin. He surely was in bad shape.

In the truck two more bodies were stacked on top of each other. Those guys were in worse shape. One guy had a series of cigarette burn marks all over his face to go with the scars he already had and even one of his eyes was burned out by a cigarette. The other guy had a mouth full of shattered teeth that resemble the crags around a deserted island.

"Ssshhh. You're gonna have plenty of time to talk my friend, plenty of time. For now, just enjoy the peace and quiet. It's probably gonna be the last time you experience it."

1 Year later

On the beautiful shores of the port city of Makarska, Croatia a wedding soiree is taking place on the roof of an illustrious building overlooking the bay and its stunning aqua tinted, crystal clear waters.

Politicians, hedge fund babies, military generals, treasury officers and a whole host of important people are in attendance. Off in the corner seated at a small square tiled table, hidden away under a large tan umbrella, sat two gentlemen adjacent from each other. Both men's security details were flanking them.

The one man was an Iranian government official, and the other man was Mr. Nobody. Mr. Nobody and the Iranian tapped their shot glasses on the glass tabletop before shooting back the spicy alcohol.

The Iranian knew that Mr. Nobody would be in attendance at this event and scheduled a meeting to discuss future plans. They reveled in each other's company while Mr. Nobody's new love interest sat on his lap seductively twirling his now shoulder length hair between her immaculately manicured nails as she whispered naughty words in his ear.

The men reached the portion of the conversation that only required the ears of those privy to the business. At that point Mr. Nobody instructed his lady friend to join the party, to dance and enjoy herself but not too much. He would join her once business was concluded. She gracefully smiles at the Iranian before excusing herself to the dance floor.

Not long afterwards the business was handled, payment and fees were addressed, when Mr. Nobody, alone, received a call to his cellphone. That was strange because no one knew his number and he place outgoing calls only. Reluctantly he answered.

He was silent at first, not wanting to reveal who he was by simple voice recognition alone.

War speaks, "Been a minute. I started to think I'd never hear from you again. You don't call. Shame on you. And I thought we were friends."

"Who is this? You must be very clever, very lucky or unlucky, for that matter, to have discovered this number."

"Oh yea. It took a lot of brain power, man hours and bullets to track you down. You spread like cancer throughout the world but today was my lucky day, so I guess you're right."

"Yea, and why is that?" Mr. Nobody asked, getting irritated.

"Because you're possibly going to be the last person, I ever have to kill again then I'll be free. My sister will be too. You know, I don't appreciate you still coming for her after almost 2 years. Says a lot about you. Breakups were hard on you as a kid, huh?"

"Who is this? I've killed entire cities, to remember a specific person would mean you meant something to me and very little people actually do."

"C'mon man you forgot your old buddy, Warren? What about William? You remember him? Sure you do. You sent a death squad to kill us. Failed with me but you succeeded with my brother. I said to myself I would hunt you to the ends of the earth for that. And I did."

Mr. Nobody chuckled, "Who?? I've killed so many men, women, and even children that I have one hell of a long list of forgotten names and faces."

Silence.

"I fucked your wife. And she screamed my name every time she had an orgasm. She said she had never been fucked like that before in her life, go figure. You shot her in the head for it. Rich losers usually lose their girls to guys like me. It happens."

Mr. Nobody swirled his trigger finger around the rim of a whiskey tumbler when War explained who he was. Instantly Mr. Nobody remembered him, and vividly. He had to maintain his composure as he spoke.

"Oh, the arrogant little shit that fucked one of 30 sluts I dealt with. So what. She cost me a few million dollars. Pennies to me, but what did she cost you, War?"

"Everything. I cashed it all in. For you. For this one moment in time. Nice suit, by the way. You always had a knack for dressing. Kudos to the new lady in your life as well. She's nice. Columbian? Ecuadorian? Yea…that's it. She's hot. Definitely an upgrade. You think she's into mid-range millionaire Black American men? Eh, I'll ask her later."

Mr. Nobody's body language changes. He shifted from relaxed to an on edge posture as he sits up in his chair.

"Ahtat. Stay seated. This won't take long. I just wanted to thank you. You showed me the best in me. Granted, the road to this higher self was some of the most fucked up terrain I've ever endured. But you showed me what I had to give to this world. What truly matters and I'm a better man for it."

Mr. Nobody suddenly relaxed as if he remembered some super special safeguards he put in place before the event. He swirled around the drink in his glass and smiled to himself.

"War, I know you're upset about …"

A single shot across the bow and the glass in his hand exploded like a lit firecracker.

"Upset? No, I bypassed the upset phase straight to God level wrath. But then I had a breakthrough. I've always been the bad one. The hardheaded one. Had to lose a lot to see the bigger picture and finally I did. I used to not want to live. I just existed and now I have a reason to do more than just exist. Now, if you will, let's get on with the next part of this."

"Even if you do succeed in killing me, they'll always be someone like me in this world because there's always going to be a need for someone like me to do the things that need to be done to progress society forward."

As Mr. Nobody spoke his woman friend danced carefree only yards from him. She twirled and swayed her beautiful petite but well balanced frame like that of a ballerina. She winked at her lover who returned the flirtatious gesture with a nod of the head and a quaint smile.

"You might be right. But this world has never had a deterrent like me before."

Mr. Nobody attempted to spring up out of his chair and escape death's grasp. But from 300 yards away concealed beneath a line of blankets and bed sheets, air drying in the sun, hid War. He was completely undetectable by Mr. Nobody's guards and personnel. Proned out, straddling the shoulder stock of a precision customized 22 caliber long rifle with a Leupold scope, silencer and bipod system making it a bulletproof platform that shoots long and true. The cartridge fed weapon was already charged and ready to fire. He switched the safety off and moved his finger to the trigger.

War whispers, "This one's for you, big brother... One to the head, one to the heart..."

Twenty-two caliber rounds already register lower than other calibers on the decibel meter but .22 Subsonic LR pushing through a 6 inch long suppressor sounds like an infant's soft breath.

The weather was warm, seasonably warm but not intrusive. Almost no breeze. Just the right conditions for a skilled shooter to make such a shot from such a great distance. The bullet's trajectory is accurate, it's spiraling precise. On a good day anyone with sharp vision could watch the bullet's path of travel to its intended target with ease.

The tiny round ruptured Mr. Nobody's skull cavity just above the ear canal. The lethal wound was concealed under layers of wet slicked back hair and the second shot was placed right of the center sternum, in the space between the third and fourth ribs, punching a neat bloodless hole in his maroon dress shirt. The thumping of those rounds colliding with him causes his body to rattle and jerk as if he were dancing to the beat. His lady friend saw the rhythmic movement and assumed her lover had finally concluded business and was ready for the pleasure portion of the evening. She danced her way to him seductively unaware she was attempting to seduce a corpse.

She dragged her hand over his chest and around his neck as she rounded his chair. The slight smirk on his face enticed her further. She traced his neckline up to his ear, swirling a frosted fingertip around his earlobe before she raked 4 fingers through his raven colored hair. She noticed moisture on her fingers that felt sticky to her. When she withdrew her hand, her palm was covered in blood.

Instinctively she shoved him away and his body flopped limply onto his belly. His shades bounced off and tumbled away revealing lifeless gelatin eyes locked into a dead far away stare.

Her scream was heard even as War was scaling down the access ladder on the side of the building he was perched from. The rifle he'd utilized for the operation was modified to detach at three places making it compactable and easy to store away in a carrying case or a simple backpack.

War blended in looking like the average run of the mill tourist, with a floral linen shirt, khakis, sunshades and backpack in tow as he paced to a car that awaited him in the nearby alleyway.

Once in the car he put it in drive and pulled off but stopped before entering the intersection, to give way to emergency service and the local police department who were speeding by going the other way.

He glanced to his right at a familiar face. Will was sitting in the passenger seat with almost an identical outfit on but wearing shades. He looked over at his little brother and smiled. It wasn't a gesture of content, more like the smile of relief. War smiled and nodded back at his twin.

He checked the route left to right one more time, noticing that his brother no longer sat in the passenger seat, he was alone. He smiled to himself. A right blinker indicated the direction he would be headed in but coincidentally it would also serve as an omen for things to come should he chose to take that route.

A harmless man is not a good man.
A good man is a very dangerous man, who has that voluntary control.
-Dr. Jordan B. Peterson